DREAMWORLD

Dreamworld

Magda Herzberger

Illustrations by
Monica A. Wolfson

Austin, Texas

Dreamworld

By Magda Herzberger

1st World Library
an imprint of
Groundbreaking Press
8305 Arboles Circle
Austin, TX 78737
512-657-8780
www.groundbreaking.com

Library of Congress Control Number: 2008941356
ISBN: 0-9793542-4-2

First Edition

Senior Editor
Barbara Foley

Book Design & Production
M. Kevin Ford

Cover Design & Production
M. Kevin Ford

Cover Illustrations
Monica A. Wolfson

Interior Illustrations
Monica A. Wolfson

Dedication

My book is dedicated
To my beloved family:
My husband, Eugene Herzberger, M.D.
Our son Henry
Our daughter Monica
Our grandchildren, Nathan and Mira Ma
As well as to my friends and readers who have supported me
With sincere love and enthusiasm.

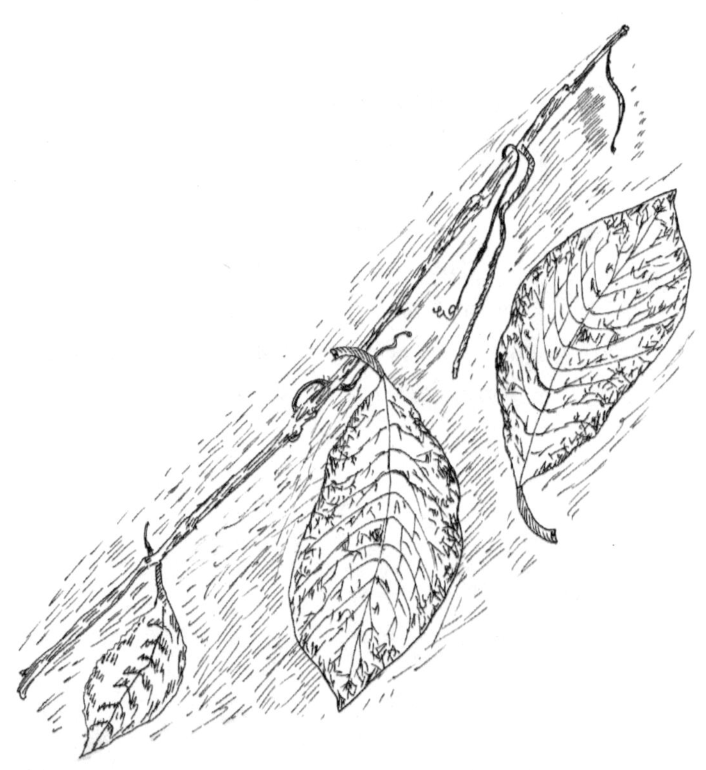

Acknowledgements

I owe a deep debt of gratitude to my beloved husband,
Eugene Herzberger, M.D.
My special thanks to my dear friend,
Maggie Smith, C.D.T.

My gratitude and appreciation to my daughter,
Monica A. Wolfson, M.E.D.T.
for all her efforts in creating and drawing the cover
and interior illustrations featured in my book.

My special thanks and gratitude to
James P. Moore, Jr., author of the highly acclaimed book,
One Nation Under God: The History of Prayer in America,
Professor at the McDonough School of Business at Georgetown University
and a former U.S. Assistant Secretary of Commerce,
for all his efforts in writing the compelling and eloquent
foreword to my book.

I am most grateful for the constant support of my publisher,
Brad Fregger, and my senior editor, Barbara Foley.

My deepest appreciation to
M. Kevin Ford
for the interior design and production of my book.

Preface

To a great extent *Dreamworld* is related to my experiences in the Holocaust. The stories in my book are based on the nightmares I had for many years after my return from the German concentration camps. As time went on my nightmares gradually subsided.

But during the night of June 17, 1981, I had a strange dream with all kinds of characters, dialogues, and action. In other words, it encompassed a whole story.

At some point in my dream the shadows of the Holocaust moved into my dreamworld in different forms, intertwining with the story of my dream, thus creating units of fiction and reality.

At my husband's suggestion I recorded my dream on my tape recorder. Then other unusual dreams followed throughout the years. I continued recording, transcribing, and developing them into short stories.

After ten years, on the night of June 17, 1991, a very bizarre thing happened. Some of the characters featured in my very first short story titled, "Magic … a Dream," reappeared again in my dreamworld, creating the continuation of that very first dream I had ten years earlier.

But when I wrote it down, to my surprise, it took the form of a poetic narrative. In other words, it became a short story written in the form of poetry. In that way "The Magic Flute," my first poetic narrative, was born.

From then on I had other dreams and all of them took the shape of poetry. And so, my other poetic narratives were born.

In the course of time, gradually my book *Dreamworld*, a collection of short stories and poetic narratives, developed. I completed it in 2001 and it is now being published by 1st World Library, an imprint of Groundbreaking Press.

Magda Herzberger
January 2009

Table of Contents

Foreword

Magda Herzberger is one of those rare American treasures. Not only has she been an eyewitness to some of the most traumatic and defining moments of the twentieth century, but she has brought those experiences, along with her unique insights, to extraordinary life through her writings

Dreamworld is the latest stop in her continuing literary journey, reaching back to her childhood and spanning more than eighty years. This collection of short stories and poetry only underscores the depth of Magda's character that echoes throughout her other books. It is no exaggeration to say that she is a living study in the human graces of faith, hope, and love.

Far from being a treasury of fictional musing springing from the mind of a gifted writer, each paragraph and stanza is anchored in some real-life experiences. Always, there is some metaphor, some grounding in a past physical, intellectual, or spiritual encounter. They may be the products of dreams, but they have their basis in the reality of an incredible past.

Dreamworld is a dazzling array of fantastic tales that invite and challenge the reader to enter into a world that we would otherwise never see. They are the product of deep spiritual values, strong family ties, noble aspirations, and of course, the worst of human indignities. Each work unveils part of an overall mosaic that displays the incredible life's story of its author.

Magda's inner mettle comes through in *Dreamworld* in the ever-watched care of three angels in "Magic … A Dream" and in their return appearance in "The Magic Flute." Haunted by flashbacks of the German concentration camps she endured, Magda has thoughts of suicide as she lies next to her husband in the wee hours of the morning. Although she finds comfort in his knowing embrace, she falls back into a sleep that conjures up disturbing everyday images that are dispelled only by the intercession of celestial beings.

Clearly it is personal fortitude, which has been a hallmark of her life, that makes this piece so troubling and yet so comforting. In both works she is rewarded for her moral courage by knowing in the end that love conquers all, particularly when it comes to the unconditional love of God and her husband Gene. It is a theme that she returns to in "The Search for My True Self," a poem that speaks to spiritual transformation through the ever watchful eye of Divine Providence.

Magda's journeys into the unknown and into the soul are conveyed in a short story and then a poem, both stark reminders of the evil that exists in the world. In the first composition she finds solace in the kindness of a strange visitor and under the watchful care of her favorite prophet, Elijah. In the second, however, she is not able to shake off the specters of the past so easily as she faces the "demonic creature endowed with human feature." One can only imagine the visages of Hitler and his henchmen lurking in her mind's eye. Those ghostly visions clearly are seared into her brain, much as they are as she faces death in "Mystery" and in her "Untitled Story."

What becomes particularly telling in *Dreamworld* is Magda's boundless determination to provide a lasting legacy through her creative writing. She wants the world to know that under the most inhumane conditions, the human spirit can survive and overcome even the deepest despair. In "Strange Encounter" she finds empathy and companionship in forging the path less travelled with poet Robert Frost. In "Night Visitor," she listens to an inner voice that drives her to reappraise the twists and turns that her life and imagination have taken. Her poem, "Spiritual Conversation," makes clear that she believes whatever talents she possesses have been God-given and that "a miraculous, mysterious, powerful, persuasive Muse" is always by her side, prepared to help guide her pen.

Two of the most unusual pieces in *Dreamworld* combine narrative, short story, and poetry into one. In the first, appropriately titled "Tricks of Destiny," Magda weaves together those poignant moments in her life that have helped make her the person that she is today. They transcend both time and space. In the inner resources of her mind she encounters all sorts of kind strangers, including a curious elf. The image of an old pear tree comes alive, bringing back fresh memories of her family and the sheer glee of being a child again. The words of Hungarian and Romanian poets ring in her ears, while the piano music of Haydn and Chopin from her youth, come back to her in an instant. It becomes clear that what she has acquired during her odyssey is that most precious of treasures—wisdom.

The second work, "Thoughts on Life, Death, and Dreams," also projects the roadmap to her life. In this case her mother, her father, and her beloved uncle appear to her, and through their love she is able to put her own life into greater focus. When she awakens from her dream, she still feels their presence and inherently knows that to the end of her days they will be with her.

Despite the dark elements, which naturally pervade the dreams of Magda Herzberger, a reader never comes away with a sense of despair. There are flickers of the possible, particularly for someone so intensely endowed with faith. How else could someone have persevered against the human depravities of Auschwitz, Bergen-Belsen, and Bremen? Or returned to her homeland of Romania only to find that Fascism had been replaced by that other insidious form of control, Communism? Or spent a tortuous year in the squalid tent communities along the coastline of Cyprus awaiting emigration to the newly created state of Israel?

In her long poem, "Visions," she finds herself once again under the protection of Elijah and several extraterrestrial beings. Through her short story, "Providence," she faces the haunting visions of Irma Grese, the notorious SS guard known to history as the "blond Angel of Death," who drags Magda to the crematory and then suddenly vanishes. Elijah reappears before her, assuring her that she is safe and still alive, and with his words she begins to see the most beautiful, exotic flowers come to life along her path. Indeed, it is in "The Best Friend of Life" that one of the great secrets to her survival explicitly appears, namely hope.

While most readers of *Dreamworld* will never meet Magda Herzberger in person to feel her exceptional warmth or her penetrating eyes and smile, they can catch a glimpse of the passion she possesses through these pages. By entering her world of fantasy, one gains a very different perspective on life. If Magda Herzberger can persevere into her ninth decade, be married to the same man for over six decades, and overcome some of the greatest challenges that most human beings will ever face at the hands of others, is there not a profound message for the rest of us? Are we not able to have greater awareness in the direction of our own lives, while gaining the self-assuredness to persevere no matter what the odds?

Magda appropriately concludes her collection of intimate dreams with "Message from Heaven." Once again an angel from God intervenes along her taxing path, making her excruciating trials more bearable. After putting her worries and doubts to rest, the angel suddenly disappears and Magda reflects,

> I stood in amazement
> Wondering if what I had experienced
> Was only a vision, a strange dream,
> Or was it reality,
> Or maybe just an explainable mystery.

Well, for those of us who have shared Magda's most intimate dreams in this treasury, there may be as many questions as there are answers, but there is one overriding conclusion. No one can predict the ultimate course of his or her own Book of Life, but with the virtues of faith, hope, and love, our chances not only for survival, but for thriving and supporting those around us is increased sevenfold. Magda's great contribution is that she is showing us the way.

James P. Moore, Jr.
Washington D.C.
January 2009

The Honorable James P. Moore, Jr.

Mr. James P. Moore, Jr. is an award-winning author whose first book, *One Nation Under God: The History of Prayer in America*, was made into the film, *Prayer in America*, for public television. Mr. Moore's latest book, *The Treasury of American Prayer*, also published by Doubleday, was released in the fall of 2008.

Mr. Moore has enjoyed a varied career in government, business, and academia. He was nominated by President Ronald Reagan and confirmed unanimously by the U.S. Senate to several senior government positions, including U.S. Assistant Secretary of Commerce.

Today Mr. Moore sits as a professor at the McDonough School of Business at Georgetown University, where he teaches International Business as well as Ethics, and where he heads up an initiative on global leadership. He also serves on several corporate and nonprofit boards and is a featured guest commentator on CNBC and on other networks. His numerous writings and speeches have been translated into dozens of languages.

Dreamworld

Journey into the Unknown

My love for the outdoors and the countryside grew in the course of time. As a child I loved to walk outdoors especially in the fall and summer, looking at the trees and the changing leaves. So, one day I was out walking in the countryside. It was fall, my favorite season. I could see many leaves on the ground. All at once the wind picked them up, and they danced on the stony, earthy road I was treading. But as I was going along, enjoying that lovely scenery, it got colder and colder. The winds started to blow even more and all the leaves went flying into the air.

There were no houses around me where I could take shelter from the cold. I was inappropriately dressed for the falling temperature. But as I continued along trying to find a place where I could go in and get warm, it grew even colder. Strangely enough, the fall scene changed into a winter scene before my eyes.

As I looked up, I could see that all the trees had lost their leaves. They were now bare, and snow was falling heavier and heavier. Big flakes were coming down. The wind picked up again, and the snow grew deeper and deeper within a short period of time.

It was slow going for me as I tried to fight the cold wind and the ever deeper snow. At one point, I got terrified because I thought that if I did not find shelter soon, I would perish. The wind was blowing wildly now and the snow was coming down heavily. Barely able to see I kept trudging on.

Then, I started running in order to keep myself warm. I was running and running and I had no idea how long I would have to run, but I thought, *I can keep it up because I used to be a marathon runner and if I could run twenty-six miles nonstop, perhaps I can survive and probably it won't even take that long.*

It seemed, though, that I had been running a long time and I still could not see any shelter in sight. It was a snowstorm and the wind was pushing the snowflakes sideways. They were hitting my face and my eyes. Finally, I could detect the outline of something at a distance, but I wasn't sure what it was. I kept running towards it.

As I came closer, I realized that it was a very strange-looking building similar to one from the Middle Ages. Although it looked like a church, it didn't have all the characteristics of one. The building was made out of heavy concrete stones and looked impenetrable. Because of its massive stone doors, I wondered how I would be able to get inside. Nevertheless, I was desperate and I started banging on those heavy doors and yelling, "Please! Please! I need help! Someone help me! I am freezing cold and I need a shelter."

But it seemed that nobody heard me. Then I realized those doors reminded me of doors I had seen before. … yes, they reminded me of bunker doors in Germany where I had been taken to the German concentration camps during the Holocaust. We worked on the streets as slave laborers in Bremen, the second-largest port in Germany; it was bombed day and night. It had bunkers and shelters with heavy concrete doors. The doors did not open very easily to pressure, which was perhaps the survival factor during the terrific bombardments. We worked as prisoners there—five hundred women selected from Auschwitz—to drag the corpses of aerial bombardment victims from the streets and also to clear the ruins of the city.

I thought, *Nobody is going to hear me. I'm just going to perish here. I am going to collapse in front of this door and die.*

Then to my amazement, the heavy door gradually opened and a figure stood in the doorway. I recognized him. It was Elijah, the prophet. I grew up with the Jewish tradition and as a child I had a special fondness for Elijah. At Passover my father beautifully performed the Seder, the traditional festive celebration of one of the biggest Jewish holidays. It was a custom at the end of the ritual to leave a glass of wine on the table. When I was a child I was told that Elijah would stop by at night, bless the house and drink from the ritual cup. I believed that. In the morning I would rush to the table looking to see if the wine was still there. The wine was always gone. Wide-eyed, I would say, "Oh, Elijah was here."

Elijah looked just like I imagined that he would look in my childhood dreams. He was tall and had a long, white beard. He looked stately and wore a white robe, like the robe my father wore at the ritual performing the Seder. The Seder, which means order, was very symbolic. Remembering the Seder got me through some of my hardest times when my life was threatened in the German concentration camps. When I felt that my strength was ebbing, in my imagination I could see my father performing the Seder, and that gave me the motivation and desire to go on living. As in a dream, I could see Elijah visiting and blessing our house. I wanted to live in order to see my father perform that beautiful Seder ritual again—but my father was killed in the camps and so it was never to be.

I was very surprised when Elijah actually appeared at the door and I knew in my heart that it was a good sign. He was wearing a golden chain with a golden key attached to it. Elijah looked at me and I said, "Oh, you must be Prophet Elijah, who came and blessed our house every year at Passover. Please help me now, I am desperate. Please give me shelter."

Elijah looked at me and said, "Come in, my child." I went in and I could see that the building from the inside didn't look like it did from the outside. It no longer reminded me of the Middle Ages because it looked like a big house with several floors and the lower part was like a corridor. From this corridor I could see some doors on the left and on the right, and there was a staircase going up to the other floors, perhaps about three.

I said to Elijah, "I would like to go into one of the heated rooms so that I can warm up."

Elijah said, "All of these doors are locked. You should know that. But I am going to give you this golden key which will open the right door for you." He placed the golden key in my palm and then disappeared.

The key looked like one which could open all the doors, like the master key in a hotel. That's what I was thinking. But this wasn't the case. At first I tried the doors on my right, but the key didn't open any of them. Then I tried to open the doors on the left, but nothing opened. I ran upstairs, shouting, "My God, all the doors are locked." But I thought, *I should go down and check again—I might have missed a door downstairs.*

I ran downstairs and noticed a door at the end of the corridor that I had not tried before. It had a different color—it was painted white. I couldn't understand why there would be only one white door and all the other doors had the natural wood color. I asked myself, *How come I missed this one?* My thoughts were that probably in my desperation, I was running back and forth and I didn't pay enough attention because I was so stressed out. I inserted the golden key in the door lock; I turned it to the left and the door opened.

Stepping inside, I found myself in a long corridor which looked like an art gallery with no pictures on its walls. It was heated and the warmth felt good to my chilled body. There wasn't any furniture around, not even a chair to sit on. Nevertheless, it was a cozy place where finally I could warm up. I wondered if I should stay there for awhile.

But then as I looked, I noticed one picture on the wall which wasn't there when I entered the corridor. Wondering how the picture got there, I decided that probably I was so desperate to find shelter that it might have been there and I didn't notice it. As I gazed at the picture, I couldn't believe my eyes. It was a charcoal sketch of my great-grandmother on my father's side whom I never knew, but I was familiar with the picture. I will never forget it because it was hanging in the living room in our home throughout the years.

I was born and raised in the northern part of Transylvania, Romania in the capital city of Cluj. When I was eleven years old the Jewish persecution started. Being Jewish meant we couldn't have a house anymore. We had to move to smaller apartments as time went on, because of the discrimination which got worse and worse. When Hitler occupied our city in 1944 we were deported to the German concentration camps. We had to leave our home and everything we had was looted. This picture of my great-grandmother was with us until that time. I grew up with it and I adored this picture through all the years of my childhood. Because she died well before I was born, I never knew her. One of my big concerns regarding our lost belongings had been this picture of her. The hunchback who did the work was a great artist, although he was never recognized as such. He worked in a small photographic shop and people would come in and ask him to draw their portraits.

To me, the portrait of my great-grandmother was full of life; her whole personality was captured in it. I liked to look at it at different stages in my life as I was growing up. She looked so pretty, even though she was not that young anymore. Perhaps she was in her fifties at the time when her picture was drawn. She had a distinguished look about her and she had a hairdo which actually looked like the hairdo I am wearing now. She had long hair and it was put up in a big bun and fastened with numerous hairpins. Many people have told me that I have a great resemblance to her and perhaps it is because of our similar hairdos and facial features. Although I never knew her, through that picture I felt that she was living with us in our home.

When I came back from the German concentration camps in 1945, I found out that fortunately my mother had survived. Much of my family had been killed, including my father. Sadly, we never found that picture of my great-grandmother. Maybe somebody wanted the attractive frame, what else? They could not relate to the picture of my great-grandmother and they might have just discarded it in the garbage can. The thought of that terrified me.

But now, there it was—I had finally found the picture and I was so happy. I kept on savoring it like I was still not convinced that it was real. The picture definitely looked real. But a strange thing happened. As I gazed at it, my great-grandmother's face seemed to come alive and she was smiling at me. She was wearing a high-necked dress with a collar and big sleeves. Then she lifted her arm and made a sign—she beckoned to me with her index finger.

It was bizarre, yet it delighted me. On the other hand, I wondered what was happening to me. *Do I see things that don't exist? Am I losing my sanity? Am I hallucinating?* But I didn't care because it made me so happy to see my great-grandmother come alive that nothing else mattered.

Then, not only was she beckoning to me, but her lips started moving and she was talking to me. She said, "Come here, my great-granddaughter. I know that you always liked me. Many times you wanted to know me, and now you have a chance to do it."

I said, "It's true! It's true, Great-grandmother! I can't even remember your name."

She said, "It's not important what name I have, but here I am talking to you."

"Great-grandmother, I always admired you and wanted to know you. I felt so sad when we lost the picture of you. It was the only thing which connected me to you."

"I know how you felt. We are going to make up for it now." She asked, "Do you really want to know me?"

"Yes! I want to know you. I want to come close to you."

She said, "Then look behind my picture. Lift it up a little and at the corner of the frame there is a button. Push this button and behind my picture you will see a secret door."

I pushed the button and a secret door opened, and I found myself in a huge room. It looked like a ballroom in another century. I saw dancers—men and women in pairs. They were wearing their rococo outfits and wigs on their heads. There was beautiful music performed by someone playing the piano. Although I wasn't familiar with that music, because people were waltzing I wondered, *Is that the waltz of Johann Strauss? And who is playing the piano so beautifully? Who is the artist?* I walked through the crowd, but it seemed that nobody paid attention to me. I could see the black grand piano. And at the piano, my great-grandmother was playing.

I thought, *Oh my God! My great-grandmother is here!* I remembered that black piano that was in the house of my grandparents. I recollected the times when I was only three years old and I had gone with my parents to my grandmother's house. As soon as we arrived, I would run to the piano room. I played children's songs and tried to compose my own compositions. Sometimes I would stay there for hours and no one could take me away from the piano. They had to come in several times and would practically have to pull me out from that piano room. I remembered pleading with my parents to let me take piano lessons. But at that time there was a belief that children at an early age should not be burdened with too much mental work. They should enjoy their carefree childhood. It was considered detrimental to teach a child an instrument at an early age.

As time went on and I became a teenager, I finally convinced my parents—actually my uncle, who was the fencing champion of Romania (he was killed in the camps, too)—to find a piano teacher for me. He found the best teacher for me—an artist, a concert pianist from age twelve. Because he was Jewish, they wouldn't let him perform anymore in concerts and he had to make a living by giving piano lessons. But that grand piano evoked in me memories from childhood when I had listened to one of my aunts so beautifully playing the piano. I could listen for hours to the music.

And now there was this beautiful music and my great-grandmother was playing. I went to her and exclaimed, "Nobody told me that you were a concert pianist!"

"You'll find out more about me now."

"Will you teach me to play? You play so beautifully."

She said, "Now I have to play for these people who are dancing. Why don't you mingle with them and find somebody, a partner? Go on now and meet some people."

I tried to do that. I went to a couple and asked, "Could you please find me a partner? Is there anyone who would like to dance with me?"

The dancing couple looked at me. I asked them, "Why am I not noticed? Why doesn't anyone pay attention to me?"

They both told me, "Look at yourself. Look at the way that you are dressed and look at us. You don't belong here. You are not one of us."

"But I want to be one of you. I want to stay here. My great-grandmother is here playing the piano and she's one of you, so I must belong to you, too. I must belong to this place."

"No, you don't. Besides, you are out of place. You are from another age. You don't belong here."

I tried to convince the man and the woman that I could be one of them if they would help me. I could be helped to be dressed like them, if that was the requirement, if my attire was disturbing. Otherwise, I tried to explain that I was a human being as they were and that we had something in common. "Is it so important the way I am dressed? That should not make a difference."

They said, "But it does make a difference because you can never be like one of us."

"What do I have to do to belong?"

"You have to be born in our century. That's where we belong. But you are an outcast. We don't want you here, and we ask you—please leave and find the place where you truly belong."

Then I was practically guided out—thrown out, in other words—and I was very upset because I couldn't even go back to talk to my great-grandmother. Unsure where I should go from there, I decided to walk up another flight of stairs. I said to myself, *On the third floor there should be a place where I belong. Perhaps that's where I will be accepted.*

I ran up to the third floor and I had the same experience—all the doors, except one, were locked. So again, I could open only one door with my golden key.

When I opened that door I saw a similar scene, only the people looked different. They were dancing to a different tune. My great-grandmother wasn't at the piano. There wasn't even a piano playing anymore. It was weird music and I wondered what instrument was playing. I could not identify it because it sounded to me, strangely enough, like a music box. I thought that maybe it was one of those upright player pianos. I looked around, but I could not see anything and I wondered where the music came from. It was very strange because I could not see a musical instrument in sight, nor could I see a music box, and yet the room was filled with music—not music that I really cared for. It didn't have beautiful melodies; it didn't have the great spiritual strength of Beethoven. This was not music of the eighteenth-century or sixteenth-century composers; it was totally unfamiliar to me.

The dancers were keeping the rhythm of the music and yet, there was something peculiar about the way they were bending their bodies. Finally I realized there was a stiffness about them even in their facial expressions. I figured, *Maybe it is only because I'm reading too much into this. Perhaps I have to get familiar with these people. Perhaps I will understand the music if I know where it comes from or what it is.*

I accosted a dancing pair and asked both of them, "Where am I? Down on the second floor I was practically thrown out. I came up here hoping to meet with friendliness. Will I be accepted here?"

At first, there was no answer. It almost seemed like they were ignoring me. As I looked around, I noticed that no one else paid attention to me either. I thought, *This is a repetition of my experience from before.*

I asked the couple again—they were the only ones who seemed willing to talk to me, "May I stay here and find myself a partner to dance with?"

Again I was told, "You don't belong here. I don't know how you got here, but you are not one of us."

I said, "I am a human being. I tried to explain down on the second floor that we have things in common like all human beings. Why doesn't anyone want to accept me?"

They said, "Look around. There's a question whether we are human beings."

"What do you mean? You look like human beings."

"Did you notice something about us which bothers you?"

I said, "Not really."

"Come on, come on. If you want to be one of us, we want to hear your opinion about us."

"I noticed some kind of stiffness in your movements. It's no wonder, I don't know how long you have been dancing this dance. Perhaps all of you have been dancing for hours here and you are tired."

The couple said, "No, you might be surprised and shocked to hear that we are not human beings."

"How come you are not human beings?"

"We are actually robots. You don't belong here. You are a human being and we are robots. We are programmed."

"I can't believe it."

The man, who looked like a young man with dark hair, very dark eyes, and nicely built body, said, "You really want to find out about us?"

I said, "Yes."

He said, "I can prove we are robots." He opened his jacket, pulled it aside, and opened the buttons on his shirt. I could see that he looked like a mechanical robot figure, indeed, run by some kind of gadget.

I was horrified. Then everybody was against me. All the people dancing in the ballroom were yelling, "Get out of here! We don't want you here! You don't belong here!" I was thrown out from that room, too.

I was getting chilly again and I found myself in another corridor on the third floor. As I looked around, I noticed that this corridor was different. There were more doors now that hadn't been there earlier, doors I had not yet tried to open. I thought, *How come I always open the wrong doors? What is wrong with me? Perhaps I don't pay enough attention. Maybe I am so obsessed with the idea that I want to belong somewhere that in the process, I lose my good judgment and I am guided by my emotions and not by my reason.*

I tried to open the doors which I hadn't noticed before but I had the same problem—my key didn't fit in any of them.

Finally my eyes fell on a door at the far end of the corridor. It had a white background and there were paintings on it. There was a picture consisting of two fruit trees and birds painted with beautiful vibrant watercolors.

I thought, *This door is familiar; I have seen it before.* Then it dawned on me—*This looks like the entrance door of our former residence.* The difference was that our residence door looked like that on the inside, not the outside. It also had a white background with the picture of two fruit trees and birds painted with vibrant colors, but the picture also included a black-and-white gate which looked like the entrance gate to a garden. The picture always reminded me of Paradise—without the presence of the Evil Snake.

I pondered, *Now the key must fit this door because this is a familiar door and this was our entrance door to our house.* I put the key into the keyhole and, indeed, it fit perfectly. I opened the door but I didn't find Paradise. Instead, I realized that I was in a jungle.

I was terrified. I wasn't cold anymore because it was pretty warm in that environment. I was totally alone in the jungle and, to my horror, I saw three mountain lions coming my way. I was sure that this time something horrible was going to happen. I realized that I had been fooled by that beautiful door, thinking that it was a good omen.

Then the lions stopped and looked at me. But one of them, the one in the middle, came forward. As she approached me, I realized that it was a female mountain lion whose photo I had seen recently in our local Arizona paper, *The Times.* I was very surprised when I read the accompanying article. They were talking about Sandy, the mountain lioness who was actually visiting our community, and in the paper were hints about what you should do when you meet Sandy. It told that Sandy had two cubs and she was circling our area. They had written, "Don't be surprised if one day you find Sandy, the mountain lioness, in your backyard." Now I hoped that she was a good-natured lioness. I was really worried because I knew that wild animals can be more dangerous when they have cubs.

As Sandy came forward, I saw that behind her had been two little cubs. But the cubs stayed with the other big lions. Sandy looked at me. I had just read in the article what you should do—the do's and don'ts when you meet a mountain lion. *First, think what you should do. Don't run—that's the worst thing you can do because they will run after you and identify you as their prey. Look into their eyes, make yourself look big, and lift your hands. Holler and scream so that you make yourself important, to show that you have power.* So I was trying to do that. I extended my arms and made myself look bigger. I looked at her and I was trying to holler, but Sandy didn't go away. She started talking to me.

"You know, I am surprised that you behave like that. I mean, why do you want to make yourself bigger? Why do you holler like that? Are you afraid of me or don't you have good manners?

I said, "Sure, I am afraid. I don't know you and I don't know what you want to do to me."

"Why are you afraid of me?"

"Because you are a wild animal and I am alone."

"Do you think that all wild animals are nasty?"

"No, I don't think so. I came initially to a three-story house, which I don't see anymore, to find shelter from the raging storm outside. I was let into that building but nobody accepted me there, and I was thrown out. Then I tried to find another place where I belonged, and I found myself thrown into this jungle. I know for sure that I don't belong here either. I am afraid you are going to kill me."

Sandy said, "Well, do you really think that I'm such a nasty lioness? I don't kill when I don't have to and, think about it, what do we do in this jungle? We kill because we want to survive, because we need food to survive."

"I hope that you're not going to eat me up."

"You really don't know this jungle. I can tell you one or two things about it. I think that many of you people are much worse than we are. We kill because we want to eat, but look what you do. You kill because you want to have power. You are making wars with each other. We are territorialists too. But each of us has a territory and we respect each other's territories. Many times in the world of human beings, territories are not respected and everybody wants the territory of the other person. For that you kill and maim."

"Sandy, I am glad that you talk that way, but if you are good-natured I really would like to have your help. Please help me to get out of here, because I really don't belong here."

"Look here, I have two little cubs and I have to take care of them. But I will help you. Before you leave, I want you to learn what it means to be an intruder in a real jungle. You are in a sort of jungle when you are in the outside world. You are in a jungle when you are in with the other human beings, a jungle of a different kind where one destroys the other—not because of lack of food, but because of the greed for power."

"Sandy, don't you have wars here?"

"Our wars here are over the fight for food. But if we have plenty of food and everyone has enough, then we don't fight for it; everyone eats his or her share of the food. We work here, too. Do you think that only human beings work hard? You are always wishing to be free and to live happily outdoors like the animals do, but don't you ever consider our hard lives? We also have to make a living by hunting for our prey. What are some of the humans doing? They hunt for pleasure and they kill us. In the jungle, more of us are killed by humans than vice-versa. We attack human beings only when we are attacked. But before you leave this place, I want you to understand us animals of the jungle. I don't want you to think that we are evil. And I want you to learn what the real jungle is like and what it means to be truly evil."

"Sandy, I'm pleased that I met you. But at this point, I still would like to get out of this jungle and find where I belong. Would you help me?"

"Yes. I can't leave the jungle because my place is here, but I will lead you out of this jungle to the gate where you can leave." Sandy led me to the gate, opened it, and let me out. Then she closed it tightly behind me and disappeared.

As I passed the gate, everything changed. I said to myself, "Finally, I came to the place where I truly belong."

I entered a beautiful forest and I saw tall maple trees. The air was pleasant. It was summer. I thought, *I am so glad to see these beautiful trees. They remind me of the Midwest where I lived so many years. They also remind me of the place where I grew up in the northern part of Transylvania, Romania, where there were beautiful forests and mountains.* So many times I wanted to see a place like that, because now we live in the desert in the state of Arizona. I also grew to like the desert and its vegetation and wildlife. We have trees, flowers, and mountains around us, but the maple trees somehow reminded me of the place where I grew up.

I was intensely happy—I felt young again. Somehow that whole environment rejuvenated me as I walked in those deep forests with many trees. I noticed a beautiful, unusually large tree. It was an apple tree. I said to myself, *I have never seen such a beautiful apple tree.* The apples were gorgeous and I wanted to pick one of them. I looked up at the tree, trying to assess how tall it was. Then I saw a figure perched up there.

The figure reminded me of Mephisto the Devil in *Faust*, the opera. He was even dressed like him, with a feather in his hat. It was strange. Then, I couldn't control myself—I said out loud, "Who the devil are you?"

Then I told myself, *I am usually very well-mannered—I didn't want to use that word, but it was a slip of the tongue.*

But the answer was, "I am the Devil. By the way, would you like to have an apple?"

I said, "Under no conditions will I have an apple from you."

"What is wrong with me? I know what you're thinking."

"How could you know what I'm thinking?"

"Because I can read your mind. You are thinking of Snow White and the Seven Dwarfs."

"No, I'm thinking of Adam and Eve in the Garden of Eden and the Snake. Under no condition will I bite into your apple."

He said, "This isn't the Garden of Eden. You are here by yourself. And by the way, I'm coming down to meet you."

He came down bringing a most beautiful apple. That apple looked just like the one which I had seen in the movie *Snow White.* The apple was plump, red, and ripe. He asked me, "Won't you have a bite of my apple? It is really good."

"Under no condition will I have a bite."

"It's not poisonous. You suspect me of putting poison in your apple?"

"I don't know, because you claim to be the Devil and you look like him, and I don't want to be tricked by the Devil."

"How did you get into this forest, into this mess that you are in?"

"Because I was looking for the right place for myself and I didn't find it."

"Do you think that you are now in the right place?"

"No. How can I be in the right place with the Devil around?"

"Don't be afraid of me. If you collaborate with me, I can help you."

"Under no circumstances will I collaborate with you and participate in your evil deeds and treacherous tricks."

"I think it might behoove you to listen to me considering in what predicament you put yourself when you entered my garden."

"Because you tricked me."

"So, am I at fault for your own stupidity and carelessness?"

"Yes, you are. If you would have put up a warning sign on your gate as follows—BEWARE THE DEVIL. DON'T OPEN THIS GATE, I would have never entered your territory."

"What do you take me for, an idiot? No one would enter Hell that way and I would run out of souls. That would be bad business for me. I would lose my reputation."

"But you must understand that considering all that, I can't trust you. Therefore, I don't want to have anything to do with you. You are fooling people like me! Why do you create such a beautiful landscape totally unfit for the gates of Hell?"

"Because I want to give the impression of being in Paradise. The beauty of the landscape has a bewitching effect. So you can feel well before you enter the fires of Hell."

"All I want is to get out of here to a place where I truly belong."

"What is wrong with being in Hell? Remember, you were once there in the concentration camps of Auschwitz in Germany. You have seen the flames of Hell."

"I was forcibly and unjustly taken there against my will, just as you lured me here with your evil tricks and deceit. I never want to be in such a horrible situation again. God saved me then and He will save me now."

"I don't think that you realize that you have to be nice and courteous to me. How else can you count on my help to let you go free? This is my domain and I am the absolute ruler of the Underground. Besides, this place is much larger than it seems and considering your bad sense of direction, you will never get out of here. Meanwhile, I can fulfill some of your wishes and dreams. First of all, I can give you youth. Considering your age, it might be beneficial to you. There are very few older women like yourself who can resist this temptation. Think of what fortunes are spent on cosmetic surgery, for anti-wrinkle creams, youth potions, and rejuvenating lotions. I can give you instant beauty. I can be the genie at your service."

"I am not dumb. I don't like the price I would have to pay for it."

"It would involve only your soul—nothing more."

"My soul is most precious to me. It belongs to my Creator at all times, both while I am alive and after I am gone. Besides, I am able to face the truth and accept the loss of my youth. The gray hair and wrinkles I gradually accumulate don't bother me. I'm not unhappy nor perturbed. The beauty of my soul is well preserved and I'm intending to keep it that way. Therefore, I don't succumb to your temptation. I don't make any deals with the Devil."

"Then I have another proposition which might be more appealing to you. It might be an interesting experience for you to see and to meet the notorious Nazi criminals; for example, Adolf Hitler, Adolf Eichmann, Dr. Josef Mengele, Irma Grese, Rudolf Ferdinand Hoess, Josef Kramer (the Beast of Bergen-Belsen), Dr. Karl Klauberg, and Mary Mendel. All of them are in Hell. Would you like to know what became of them?"

"I can forego my curiosity. I hope that they were burned in Hell."

"Not exactly. You will see what happened to them if you come with me for a visit to Hell."

"You can't tempt me with anything. As I told you before, I don't make any deals with the Devil."

"Don't you understand that if you don't make any deal with me, you will never get out of here? You are in my power and under my spell. Be reasonable. We can make an agreement whereby I state that you are only a visitor in Hell for the sole purpose of seeing the fate of the infamous Nazi criminals who killed your father and many members of your family, and who were responsible for killing six-million Jews like you. You are a survivor. They almost killed you, too. If we come to some kind of agreement, I will help you to get out of here."

"I don't trust you, but I realize that I'm in your grip. But if I have to make any deal with you in order to obtain my freedom, I want to maintain my rights, too. You have to accept my demands and sign your name under mine. You have to agree that if I go for a visit to Hell for the sole purpose mentioned above, I will not become an inmate and that you promise to set me free."

"Who is your lawyer here? What are you talking about? I alone make all the laws. You still don't understand that you are under my power and spell. I don't ever sign my name for any of my business deals, and I'm not doing it for you either. Who do you think you are? I'll tell you who you are. You're a powerless human being at my mercy, lost in my domain."

"That's what you think. I am not helpless. One thing I know is that a greater power is ruling over you. God is my protector. Being Jewish, I am a member of His chosen people. He liberated me from the Hell of the Holocaust and He will free me from here, too. I have the Shield of David with me. I always carry it along. Look, it is hidden here under my garment." I pulled out the Star of David and put it in front of the Devil's eyes. I didn't know for sure if it would work. I knew that his power diminishes if you show him the cross. But to my surprise, the Devil became more and more humble. I could see him trembling and his might diminishing. "Do you agree to put your signature accepting my terms if I make an agreement with you?"

"You just told me before that you don't trust me. Aren't you afraid that I will trick you?"

"No. Because if you break the rules of our agreement, then you'll have to deal with God and your punishment will be great. I know that you fear only God. You will be locked in your Hell forever and you will never be able to face the world. You will be banished forever from the face of the earth. Indeed, that would please me. It would be wonderful if that evil spirit of yours would not exist anymore."

"I will always exist as long as mankind lives on Earth. A certain amount of evil is built into every human soul. Only the degree of it varies. There is no total purity in any of you humans. You consider yourselves the superior race. You trick each other, tear each other apart. Treachery, deceit, envy, greed, jealousy, cruelty, brutality, and passion for power are among the human traits. Think of the crimes some of you commit. Your prisons are filled with criminals. As you can see, nobody can annihilate me. Angels live in Heaven, and I live on Earth and beneath it. The Devil existed even in Paradise. How else could Adam and Eve taste the forbidden fruit and be banished from there? Even the Angels in Heaven didn't observe me being there. As you can see, I am clever and cunning.

"How do you explain that temptation existed even in Heaven ever since Man was born? But how else could Mankind itself be born if Adam and Eve would not have tasted the Fruit of Knowledge? How else would people multiply? So, you see, I will never die. I am tolerated to a certain extent even by the Ruler of the Sky. But I have to admit that I have my limitations. God has power over me; therefore, I will sign my name accepting your conditions. This time you tricked me; therefore, you are not welcome to stay for long in Hell. You are too close to God and I don't like that. I will help you and I will take you out of here and liberate you from Hell. But no matter how cunning you think you are, you have to realize that you are still under my spell and, therefore, for now you have to follow me to Hell."

I walked with the Devil. We passed a beautiful forest with its tall, hard maple and oak trees. I felt the intoxicating, sweet fragrance of wild flowers in the air. I noticed some beautiful red roses emerging from the tall grass.

After awhile, the landscape changed. We were treading on a bare, rocky surface. The outline of a big building gradually appeared. It looked like a huge castle with high towers carved out of heavy boulders. From its large chimneys huge flames were belching and the air was filled with a strange, sickening, sweetish odor of burning flesh. It reminded me of the crematories of Auschwitz. The Hell of the Holocaust was facing me. The heavy stone entrance door was locked. It had a sign on it: "The Ports of Hell."

The Devil opened the door with his key. We entered a large office with an enormous desk placed in the center of the room. To my horror and outrage, Adolf Hitler was sitting behind it. There was a big stack of files placed in front of him. There were a number of other desks placed all along the right and the left sides of Hitler's desk. I recognized the infamous Nazi criminals sitting behind them: on the right—Adolf Eichmann, Heinrich Himmler, Dr. Josef Mengele, Irma Grese, Dr. Fritz Klein, and Dr. Karl Klauberg; on the left—Rudolf Ferdinand Hoess, Josef Kramer (the Beast of Bergen-Belsen), and Mary Mendel.

I asked the Devil, "What are these monsters doing here?"

The Devil answered, "They are my most important collaborators. They have the highest positions in Hell."

"How come they earned so many privileges, so much distinction here? They should have been burned in the fires of Hell a long time ago. I am a Holocaust survivor. They deserve the highest punishment for the murder of six-million Jewish people."

"But where will I find more suitable evil souls to work for me in Hell?"

"What exactly are they doing here?"

"Whatever they did in the concentration camps of Germany when you were their prisoner. They torture, experiment, and burn the souls. I find them very helpful."

Suddenly, I saw all of them looking at me and smiling, and telling the Devil, "So, finally you brought us this last Jew? We have been waiting all these years to have one to play with. We have to think of all the methods of torture which were perfected throughout the past years. We will apply the best torture devices before putting her in the furnace. We haven't seen a Jew in a long time, so let's try to make the best of this one at hand."

"Do you think that I am the last Jew on Earth? I have to inform you that you couldn't annihilate all of us. Some of us, like myself, survived and we have many generations of living Jews."

"Yes, but we didn't manage to kill you in the camps so we are going to do it here!"

Then the Devil picked up the conversation and intervened, "You can't do that no matter how strong your desires are. You are dead souls. You lost your power to harm any living outsider."

"But you have the power to do it," they said unanimously.

The Devil looked at me with a friendly smile. I detected a mischievous glimmer in his eyes. "Ignore them," he said. "Come with me now to our big furnace. Would you like to see who will burn there next?"

At this point, I became suspicious of his intentions and I pulled out again my Star of David and pointed at him. "No tricks. Remember, God is with me. I am one of His chosen people."

I barely finished my sentence when a terrific rumble was heard, followed by a powerful, sharp, whistling sound—similar to the sound of a falling bomb before hitting its target. Then, a big detonation took place not too far from where I was standing. A part of the thick wall of the chamber was torn out by an invisible force, providing for me an opening through which I could run for safety.

As soon as I was outside, I saw a raging fire descending upon the Nazi criminals. The huge flames engulfed and consumed their wicked souls. I could see the Devil shaking, trembling with fright and disappearing.

I heard a voice telling me, "Don't fear the Devil anymore. God is with you." Elijah was standing in front of me. I was so happy to see him. I remembered that the golden key he gave me was still in my pocket where I placed it when I entered the garden of the Devil. I pulled it out and wanted to return it to him, but he said, "Keep the key. It might still be useful to you."

I asked him, "Did I fail to use this key in the right way all along? It seemed like I always opened the wrong doors with it and I ended up in the wrong places where I didn't belong. I don't understand why I made the same mistake over and over again."

"There were no mistakes, no errors made by you. You were guided by the invisible hands of Destiny and you opened the doors leading into the mysterious world of the unknown. You could not prevent or foresee the many unexpected surprises, mysteries, and miseries planned for you secretly. You got lost during your adventurous and mystical journey into the unknown."

"Elijah, I am so confused and tired. I don't know anymore where to go or where I truly belong. I have lost myself. Please help me and advise me what to do."

"I came here to help you. Come along with me and I will take you on a different, more pleasant journey."

I felt safe and secure walking with Elijah. I knew that he would finally take me to the right place and show me the right direction.

We walked together silently for a long time it seemed. We passed the green meadows scattered with blooming wild flowers. We crossed a forest of birch trees. We wandered through the tall, majestic evergreens. We ventured deeper and deeper into the woods until we came to a clearing. From there we followed a narrow foot trail flanked by huge flowering linden trees. Their blossoms emitted a strong, pleasant, sweetish fragrance in the air. At the end of the trail we came to a small, simple cottage looking like a log cabin.

Suddenly, Elijah disappeared and I was alone wondering where I was and why Elijah had vanished. I could see an iron gate leading to the entrance door of the cottage. It was late afternoon. The sun was setting and it was getting very cool. I decided to get inside the cottage since I did not want to spend the night outdoors in that remote, solitary place. Luckily the iron gate was unlocked. I passed through it and stood at the front entrance of the cottage. It looked deserted.

I knocked on the door but no one came. It seemed nobody was inside. Turning the knob, I found the door was locked. Now, I was getting worried. Once again, I felt abandoned. There was no sign of Elijah. Then I remembered the golden key in my pocket. I also recalled Elijah telling me it might still be useful. Maybe this was why he didn't want me to return it to him.

I hoped that my key would open the cabin door and finally I would find where I belonged. What other unpredictable surprises and adversities were waiting for me behind the door? Nevertheless, I felt that I had no choice. I placed the key into the keyhole. It fit perfectly, and I turned the knob slowly and opened the door.

The cottage appeared much bigger from outside than from inside. It contained only one small room. The only furniture in it was a large desk with a swivel chair behind it. Strangely, it looked just like the desk and chair in my study at our home. On the desk were a big stack of papers, an oil lamp, a small container filled with ink, and a quill pen. I was surprised to see a modern desk with all those old-fashioned items on it. I was suspicious, wondering about the meaning of all that.

I locked the door behind me to assure my privacy. Next, I sat down at the desk. Since it was getting dark, I wanted to light the oil lamp, but there were no matches around. I felt exhausted. Closing my eyes, I waited for the appearance of Elijah, but he did not show up. Hopeless and depressed, I put my head down on the desk and fell asleep.

I couldn't tell how long I slept, but when I finally opened my eyes, I could see that somebody had lit the oil lamp for me. My first thought was that probably Elijah was there with me. But as I raised my head I saw an angel standing before me. The body and face of the angel were covered by an opaque, thick, silky veil. Only two, large, extended wings were showing.

I was speechless, filled with consternation, looking at the strange heavenly apparition. "Who are you and how did you get in here? Where am I?"

"I am the Spirit of Creativity. I got in here with my golden key which is just like yours. You are in the Spiritual Sanctuary. This is the place of your destination. You belong to the world of fantasy and imagination."

"Who am I?"

"You are the poet. I am your inspiration. I have known you for thirty-seven years, ever since you wrote your first poem. I was at your side all this time."

"Why didn't you manifest yourself? Why did it take you so long to appear before me?"

"I was your silent, invisible, loyal companion. We always communicated with each other at this spiritual station."

"And why have you revealed yourself to me at this time?"

"Because I couldn't let you lose your spiritual self. I wanted to remind you who you are. You are a writer. See the papers and pen next to you? Pick up your pen and write."

"I can't do it. I'm tired, depressed, and lonely. I have no imagination. I can't write anymore."

The Spirit of Creativity disappeared, but nevertheless I sensed the presence of my true, loyal, ethereal friend. I knew that my silent and devoted companion was still with me in the room. I heard her voice telling me, "What are you waiting for? Pick up your pen and write."

A sheet of paper was placed before me by an invisible hand. The same hand lifted the quill pen, dipped it into the ink, and placed it between my fingers. And I began to write.

Strange Visitor

The Spirit of Poetry
Came to me
Long ago,
To reveal the many wonders
Of the mind,
Helping me to find
The road to eternity …

At our first encounter
I was distrustful,
Encompassed by fear,
Bewildered and shy,
Pondering why
Did this mysterious specter
Suddenly appear,
Like an angel
Sent from the sky …

Since then,
My life has never been the same …
Strange apparition,
I know your name,
Miraculous Muse!

You opened my heart,
Planting into it
The magic seeds of inspiration …

You penetrated my spirit
Starting its revolution,
Bringing forth new thoughts
And evolution …

Who sent to me
This friend of my soul
Who guides my thoughts
And leads the path of truth,
Who holds within
Her mystic shrine
The sacred power
Of youth?

Journey into the Soul

Where are today
The sweet delightful dreams of yesterday?
Last night they pushed their way
Through the dense opaque curtains of the night
Coming into sight.

Now, in the sunlight
I search for them everywhere,
But they vanished into dawn's thin air...
They were only delusions of some kind
Of the sleeping mind.

But as my eyes wander,
I discover a strange, deformed,
Disfigured, unearthly creature,
Looking like a supernatural apparition
From a horror picture,
Hiding in the corner of my room,
Weaving a black shroud
On an ancient loom,
The symbol of death and doom.

Although I am possessed by fear,
I can't control my curiosity,
Nor the strong desire
To approach this monstrosity,

In order to see who it is, more clearly.

As I come close,
A giant purple rose in bloom
Appears in front of me,
Displayed on the palms
Of two weird human hands
Equipped with animal paws
And sharp claws.

As I cast down in awe my eyes,
I detect two sturdy purple legs
Covered with big pointed thorns
And two blue feet,
Equipped with miniature horns
Instead of toes.
Gradually, a distorted gray body
Comes into view before me.

Two large, flapping shark-fins
Stick out on each side
Of a rough, pale-nude torso.
Could this demonic creature
Be a close relative of Mephisto?
Is this real, or only a vision?
A definition of decay, madness, and atrocity?
Am I losing my reason and sanity?

I can also discern
The shadow of an ancient urn

From which hot flames are rising,
The vague contours
Of an indistinguishable face
Obscured by a dense fog
And red-burning, thick, course,
Vivid-scarlet, bloody lips
Stretched into a mocking grin,
Revealing sharp teeth
Not white, but green.

Even in my wildest dream
I have never seen
Such a horrible scene!
A crown made of glittering precious jewels
Is suspended in space,
Upon an invisible head and face.
I want to flee
From this terrible monstrosity,
But two red-glowing, fiery eyes,
Which bewitch and terrorize,
Stare at me, reflecting
Insolence, arrogance, conceit,
Cruelty, mischief, and deceit,
Scorching my body and face
With their intense heat.

I want to run, but I can't move from my place.
Feeling confused, not thinking clearly,
I stand motionlessly under their spell,
Unable to scream or yell.

I try to make a sign with my right arm,
Signalling to be left alone
And to be spared from harm.

Just then I notice
This satanic underworld creature
Is sitting on a throne
Carved out of human flesh and bone!
I start trembling like a leaf in fall,
And in my desperation
To Almighty God I call
For help and protection,
For support and affection,
Knowing that only God can break this evil spell
And save me
From this representative of Hell,
Who probably nourishes on people's blood,
Inflicting suffering, torture and grief,
Whose heart must be as cold and stiff
As the North Pole's ice,
Who surely doesn't belong
To Heaven's Paradise,
But to a ruthless world
Where there is no pity,
No kindness, no decency,
No love, compassion, or compromise.

Finally I am able to master my fear,
I hear my voice loud and clear:
Who are you, abominable creature,

Human monster of the night?
How did you survive the daylight?
Did you fight the sun's bright rays
In some unusual ways?
How did you get into my room?
Did you come in
On a witch's broom?

I am the personification and manifestation
Of your sinister thoughts,
I was born out of your fantasy and imagination.
My dear master, listen to me:
Now that I am alive and here,
I plan to stay,
You can't chase me away!
Maybe we can work together,
Like birds of a feather.
We can go through the perilous dark passage
Of suffering and pain
To be reborn again.

I have a great idea,
Come with me to the desolate island of fantasy.
There, we will cross
The dark, turbulent waters of Hades
And we will see the great flames
Of the Purgatory.
We will meet Dante
And some ancient figures

Of Greek mythology.
You always searched only
For goodness, compassion and beauty
And for the saintly attributes
Of mankind and the Universe.

But now, let us traverse
Through the ugly, heinous labyrinth
Of the King of Darkness
And see the fire of Hell,
So you can write and tell
About the duality
Of ugliness and beauty,
Of wild passion and cruelty—
All that belongs to life,
As much as peace and harmony.

Evil seducer, Devil's messenger,
Malignant creature,
Please leave me alone!
I don't have grave sins
For which I have to atone
And be subjected to suffering and torture.
Neither am I interested
To witness others' agony.
Retreat into my mind and disappear,
Because it is quite clear
That I don't desire your company.

Ignorant mortal,
My answer is no!
You might want to stay
Humble and low,
But now is the hour
To cross and to follow
The silent volcano
Of your heart,
Which can erupt at any minute.
That's where we are going to go—
Let the hot lava flow,
Witness its fiery glow!
Write and record what you see
In the deep pit of your soul
And of human nature—
Describe the many faces
Of death, destruction,
Of greed and jealousy.
Then, come back anew
And stir in yourself
The angels' food
And the Devil's brew.
This special opportunity
Is offered to very few,
And now I offer it to you.

You will also enter with me
The deep cave of dirt and grime—
Those who feed on betrayal
Think that evil is sublime.

I will not retreat into oblivion,
Nor fade into obscurity,
Until you will comply
And accept my invitation
To come with me to life's tragic station.
My home is in every person's mind,
Regardless if they are considerate or kind.
Behind each human soul
Dwells ravage, carnage, rage, envy,
Jealousy, and greed.
Travel with me at high speed.
Remember my shadow is everywhere
Where there is suffering, hunger, and despair—
Regardless if you are virtuous, wise, and clever,
My shadow is lodged in your mind forever.
You can't eradicate
The ghost of imagination and fate!

Accept the way I am,
Disfigured and slimy,
And please try to see some worth
And beauty in me—
I am also your friend,
Therefore, some attention I demand!
Look upon me
As the reminder and pathfinder
Of deceit and calamity,
And as a representative
Of unwanted reality.
Accept me as a part of life's duality.

Foul seducer, demonic creature
Endowed with human feature,
Evil teacher of suffering and torture.
As I stated to you previously,
I don't desire your company.
I will never go with you!
Let me through, heinous shadow,
Who brings upon the world
Tears, disaster, and sorrow,
Infecting and poisoning
The healthy blood's flow.
Please retreat into the flaming Hell below.
I only follow the wise,
The pure, the honest and the true—
All these qualifications certainly don't fit you!

Don't be a stupid imbecile—
Every human carries the seeds of evil
And parts of the Devil.
No one's heart is entirely pure
Or completely sterile.
Don't look for the kind
Of genuine truth and honesty
Of which most people are blind.
These special qualities are hard to find
Because they are almost extinct
On the stage of humanity,
And therefore, they are only rarely mentioned
In the books of history.

My mission and goal
Is to kill and maim,
To destroy the human body and soul,
To feed on the blood of the living,
To bring flood and disaster,
War and destruction,
To wipe out each speck of compassion,
To wreck faith and affection,
To feed on the weak,
To prey on the sick,
To ride with death
Side by side
With joy, satisfaction, and pride!

Hideous shadow,
Part beast, part man,
Lacking conscience and remorse,
Who enjoys inflicting pain
On whomever you can,
Don't ask me to follow
Your treacherous course.
Stop bringing upon the world
Tears and sorrow.
You can't exert your power
Over me for long,
I feel confident and strong.
I belong to love and honesty!

You can't sway me
From the right course,

I pick my beliefs and values
From a completely different source.
I don't ever want to belong
To the Devil's crew,
And become ruthless, cruel, and ugly like you.

No man is quite straight and honest
Or exempt from the hornet's nest.

Pathfinder of calamity,
Despiser of harmony and beauty,
Making a joke out of life, a parody,
You have no respect for life's sanctity!
You are a worshipper of blasphemy.
Go and tempt the pessimist,
The nihilist, the atheist—
I am not one of them!
Neither do I cherish or wear
Nastiness' emblem,
Or the stamp of dishonesty and shame.
You can't tempt me
With your acts of tyranny.
I want to follow my own way
And resist your temptation.
To God I pray without cessation
To give me love and faith,
To grant me peace and harmony.
God is the one who decides
The direction of my destiny!

Curb your desire
Of turning me into your prey
Because all your efforts are in vain.
You can't alter the train of my thoughts
Or diverge the routes designated for me.
Almighty God is my guide,
He is always the One
Directing my destiny!

I despise your naiveté and stupidity,
Believing that life encompasses
Only beauty and nicety.
Nothing is eternally pure and so pretty,
There is no cure for human vice,
Or for destruction and annihilation
On life's station.

I believe that for me
A peaceful and harmonious life awaits,
And not one of turbulence and rage
Or the Devil's burning cage.

Listen to me,
I am the teacher
And the true feature
Of reality,
Existing in its crude form
In every culture of mankind.
I was left behind
By a group of demons

Of a very special kind.
Come with me and face reality!

I feel chills running down my back,
I am a total wreck.
I want to recover from my daze
And snap out from my confusion,
Temptation, and haze.
Am I on the threshold of insanity?
Is there anyone who can help me?
Who can explain and clarify
What's wrong with me?
Before I crack up and die,
Before I get totally out of control
And let madness within me
Take its toll,
And fulfill the Devil's goal
To possess and torture forever
My body and soul!

Oh God, to you I pray,
Please help me and listen to my call!
Assist me to find my way,
Be my Guide, and let me decide
What is the best course for me.
Chase away this demon
Who wants to lure me
To the treacherous path
Of violence and calamity.
And let the tidal waves

Of my turbulent thoughts subside
And gently touch the smooth shore of calm,
Peace, and serenity.
My Creator and Protector,
Let me regain my composure.

I can hardly believe
What my eyes see.
The hot rays of the sun
Penetrate my room,
Chasing away my terror and gloom.
I am alone ...
I detect a huge spider
On the corner, facing my bed,
Spinning its delicate net
From a silver thread.

Am I dreaming
Or am I awake?
Or is this new vision just a fake?
In the intricate web
A horrified big fly is waiting
For the fatal stab.
This isn't the terrifying creature
I have seen before
So I don't have to worry anymore.

But then, just as I am ready
To pursue my routine daily chore,
I see the fiery glow

Of two red eyes,
And in horror I realize
That this insignificant creature
Doesn't belong either
To Heaven's Paradise.

Is this another manifestation
With all the characteristics
Of the one before?
Is there another nightmare
For me in store?
I don't understand anything anymore!

Dreamworld

48

Magda Herzberger

Magic . . . a Dream

I had a strange dream in the early morning of June 17, 1981. I had tossed and turned all night, haunted by unpleasant memories. I had checked the clock every fifteen minutes, watching the hours pass, unable to relax. As the night wore on, I got more and more anxious. The more uneasy I became, the less chance I had to induce sleep.

By 3:30 in the morning, I was extremely restless, filled with anxiety, and terribly depressed. I even had suicidal thoughts. This deep depression was hovering over me, taking away all peace of mind.

I knew I was fighting unresolved problems within me. I was trying to get rid of painful memories from the past which were still haunting me. The wounds of suffering and disillusionments which I carried through the years within myself were deeply etched in my mind. Their harmful residue was still coating my body and soul. Suddenly, all those terrible memories had surfaced again and were reactivated.

It must have been sometime after 3:30 when I finally dozed off, but only for a few minutes. As soon as I was awake, the images from the past, the painful memories, returned to haunt me.

I couldn't stand it anymore. I reached for my husband who was sleeping next to me. I said to him, "I am very depressed and suicidal. I feel that time is running out on me. I am wondering if I am that much needed on this earth." As I spoke, tears were running down my cheeks.

Then my husband gently took me in his arms. I put my head on his chest, my favorite place. I always find peace and contentment when I am lying next to him, in the warmth of his embrace. He is my man, my love. I like the soft, golden hair on his chest. Sometimes I play with it.

I was crying, and he said, "No, no, don't do that, just relax. Stay here with me." He embraced me, putting his arms around my shoulders, keeping me close to him. "Just relax, even if you can't sleep. Sooner or later, you are going to fall asleep here."

I felt sorry that I had burdened my husband, especially since it was his birthday, June 17. I recalled that he was now 61 years old. Everyone feels at a certain age, that time is running out. He had been having a very busy week, coping with heavy responsibilities, performing difficult surgical procedures. It wasn't right to burden him on this special day. I felt so guilty, yet my desire to find some relief and peace of mind was so strong that I couldn't control myself. My inner demons had become unbearable. I was just resting on his chest still agitated, still turbulent inside. I can't say at what precise moment it was when I fell into a deep sleep.

I had the strangest dream—it was so nice to have a dream. For the longest time, I couldn't remember my dreams, and dreams can be nourishing in your depressive moments. I believe that everyone of us has depressing moments, when we review our whole life, remembering past experiences and events, when we are invaded by old memories which we can't escape, when we try to face and solve difficulties.

We each have different problems and different needs, but we are the only ones who know what our needs are.

Sometimes we get confused about our needs. We may be aware that something is missing in our life, but we can't pinpoint exactly what it is.

I had been wishing that I would have a nice dream which would sustain my desire to work and to find happiness.

In my dream, I found myself in a different world, a magical world of imagination, where nothing is impossible, where images appear from nowhere and quickly disappear. There are no limitations in our dreams. We can be anywhere, anytime we want to be, without any difficulty.

It is strange that we never understand the great miracle of dreaming, yet spend so much of our life dreaming. There are so many explanations of what a dream is. Psychoanalysts interpret dreams, but no one can understand fully how dreams are conceived, how they develop a life of their own.

In my dream, I was far away from the bedroom. I was out in the countryside. It was fall and a storm was approaching. The leaves were being thrown to the ground and some of them were flying all over.

Fall always invokes in me a feeling of nostalgia. It conveys the end of something old, which becomes the beginning of something new.

Seasons follow seasons,
Generations succeed generations,
Life starts with a loud cry
And ends in a silent sigh.

There is a feeling of loss attached to autumn.

The trees lose their leaves,
The flowers shake off their petals,
Standing naked and lonely
Like deserted isles.

I also felt the strong grip of loneliness. I was alone, trying to find our parked car. I knew that my husband was around. I could see him walking down a country road, which was covered with brown grass. I called to him,

"Please come, where are you? I can't see you. It is so stormy here. Where is our car parked?"

"You know where we parked. I am running along, you can find your way."

It seemed to me that our car wasn't so far away, yet I had difficulty in finding it. The storm grew stronger and stronger. The wind was blowing wildly. I detected several houses along the countryside, and a hill. On the top of the hill sat a familiar house. I knew I had been there before.

As I approached the foot of the hill, I saw our pediatrician from Monroe, Wisconsin. So many times we had called him to treat our son and daughter in the past when they were ill. I was happy to see him. I asked him, "Can you help me, please, to find our car? I am worried about this storm. My husband went ahead, and I can't see him. I know that we were here somewhere before, and our car must be nearby."

"Oh," he said, "you are standing next to it. Look up to the top of this hill. There it is!"

"No!" I said, "It is not my husband's car I am looking for, but my car, the black Cadillac."

I tried to tell him that I had traded in my Chrysler for a Cadillac. Actually, I had traded in my Chrysler for a sports car. My husband took the sports car, and I got his car, the Cadillac. I was trying to explain to him that I was looking for that car, the black Cadillac.

He looked surprised, trying to figure out the reason for my utter confusion.

He said, "Well, can't you see that your black Cadillac is the one on the top of this hill?"

I looked up, and indeed my black Cadillac was there, but I didn't see my husband, although he was still calling me from somewhere below.

At the base of the hill, there was a road going down. His voice came from that direction. When I looked up again, the Cadillac had disappeared, and the pediatrician was gone, too. The wind continued to blow wildly.

Suddenly, I saw somebody opening one of the windows of the familiar house and looking out. It was a minister dressed in black, and he seemed to be middle-aged. He had short, light-brown hair and broad shoulders. He looked at me, and I was pleading, "Please, let me in! The wind is blowing, the sky is covered with black, ominous clouds, and I can't find my car! Can you help me, please?"

To my dismay, he shut the window and bolted the front door. I wondered what sort of a minister he was if he couldn't comfort somebody in need.

I continued to search for my car, running down the hill and shouting for my husband.

"Where are you? I can't find you!"

I heard him answer from a distance. "I am here. Just follow the path, because you know I am here, not far. You will find your way."

I ran downhill faster and faster in my desperation, but I still didn't find my husband, nor did I see my car anywhere. The wind picked up, blowing stronger and stronger.

I kept calling to my husband, "I am scared. I can't reach the car. It looks like a tornado is coming. What should I do?"

Suddenly the wind lifted me up and carried me away with great force. I was terrified. After awhile, to my surprise, the wind put me gently down on my doorstep.

It was strange that our front door was open. I was sure that we had locked it before we left. I entered our house. There was nobody inside. I figured my husband would arrive later. After all, for me it was a short distance in the air. So it was understandable that I had arrived home first. It was a natural flight on the wings of the wind, free of obstacles. Now, I was worried about my husband. *Where is he?* Knowing his good sense of direction, I felt sure that he had found the car and he must be on his way home.

I ran down the stairs leading towards our family room to see if anybody was there. The door of the room was locked. I distinctly remembered that I had not locked the door before we left. It occurred to me that maybe the door got stuck, so I pushed it really hard until finally it opened.

As I entered the room, the first thing which caught my eye was a king-size bed placed in the middle of the room. There never had been a bed in the family room. Everything that followed seemed unreal, bizarre, and frightening.

There was a woman lying on the bed, looking very ill. She was thin, pale, and middle-aged. She had long, straight, chestnut-brown hair. I felt that she was dying.

I was utterly bewildered and shocked when I noticed that two of my deceased relatives were standing next to her. The two women were my mother's cousins who had been killed in the extermination camp of Auschwitz-Birkenau during World War Two. I had seen them many years ago when they were still alive. I never imagined that I would ever see their faces again. They looked to me like weird apparitions, like insane illusions. Shivers were running down my spine.

Nevertheless, I took control of myself and I asked them what was going on.

"Well, we are comforting this sick woman," they said.

"Sick? She looks like she is dying," I replied.

"No, no," they were telling me, "she is not dying. What you see is deceptive. Just sit here with us for awhile. She is not always like this."

I sat down and looked at the woman. She was pale. Her eyes were closed. There was no color in her cheeks. She was limply stretched out on the bed, and she was covered with a white sheet. There was not much sign of life on her face. Despite all that, I sat down beside her, waiting for a miracle to happen. After awhile, I could see color returning to her cheeks and they gradually regained their fullness.

She opened her eyes. There was a spark, a liveliness in them. She sat up on the bed, and she became exuberant, even laughing and filled with the joy of life.

It was a miracle. I have always believed in miracles. I remember when I was liberated from the Bergen-Belsen extermination camps, on April 15, 1945. I was dying there and yet, miraculously, I was given a second chance.

Only in dreams can the scene change so rapidly from one moment to the next. Suddenly, this whole image disappeared. I was upstairs in our living room. I could see my daughter sitting on the sofa. I wondered how or when she had gotten into the house. She must have been waiting for me. I sat down on the sofa next to her. I was happy to see her, but gradually a terrible feeling of sadness and loneliness, almost to the point of hopelessness, descended upon me.

I could feel it in my throat and in my whole body. I felt a terrible cloud of depression surrounding me, clouding my reason. Suicidal thoughts were crossing my mind. At the point when I had my darkest thoughts, my daughter suddenly said, "Mother, I made a wish, you make one, too. I know that sometimes wishes can come true."

So, I closed my eyes. I didn't know what my daughter's wish was, but my wish was to feel joy and peace in my heart. To be like that woman whom I had seen before, who was dying in one moment and in the next one, she was lively and exuberant. I wanted to feel that elation, to have that glitter in my eyes again.

When I opened my eyes, three angels from Heaven were standing before us. One of them looked just like me when I was a teenager. They had youth and innocence. They were such a beautiful sight. They were wrapped in white veils ornamented with silver stars.

One of them, who seemed to be the oldest, had a flute in her hand. The others picked up their flutes and they performed together the most beautiful song I had ever heard.

Its melody had a magical quality. As I listened, it gradually created an exuberance and a joy in my heart. At one point, I felt that maybe my daughter took for granted this exquisite melody, because she didn't look as enthusiastic as I. Then, I wanted to express my gratitude to these angels who came from Heaven to entertain us.

I said, "Thank you, thank you for this beautiful and glorious tune."

I didn't know what my daughter's wish was at that moment. I fancied that maybe her wish was to see the three angels. My wish was to feel happiness in my heart and maybe, indeed, our wishes had come true.

My daughter urged me to ask the angels some questions concerning the origin of their beautiful musical work of art.

I timidly approached the angel who had such a similarity with me. Feeling close to her, I took the liberty to ask her to explain to me how this beautiful unearthly melody was composed.

The angel came close and said, "Do you really want to know? Then, look at my flute. The magic is in this instrument. This is not an ordinary flute."

As I looked at it closely, I noticed that it was larger than any other ordinary flute. It didn't have a round shape either. It consisted of four symmetric rectangular faces, each one of them containing many miniscule holes.

"This flute looks very strange and complicated. It must be hard to play this unusual musical instrument and to bring forth through its tiny cavities such complex melodies."

The angel replied, "The flute and the melodies you heard seem more complicated than they really are."

This magic flute made in Heaven,
Which to me was given,
Has marvelous properties
And magical qualitites.
It is endowed with a creative spirit
And with power and grit.
It has an intrinsic ability
To converge its many sounds
With simple notes,
Into a celestial melody.
It also has the capability
To transform a melodious theme
Into a complex symphony.
You can see
This mysterious instrument
With its inherent
Miraculous talent,
Only in your dream.
The flute and me
Are a part of a saintly
Musical team.

And now I am ready
To give you some instruction.

Please pay attention!
I will start with a brief lecture
On musical structure.
This knowledge is far reaching,
But in the first phase
Of my teaching,
I will play for you
A simple melodic phrase.

The angel placed the flute to her lips
And started performing.
A beautiful, haunting melody
Was gradually forming.
When it hit my ears,
It brought to my eyes
Torrents of warm tears.

While the angel was playing,
The flute was slowly turning
From side to side,
In a continuous, circular motion,
In a controlled, soft, smooth glide,
Keeping a steady pace,
Moving with ease and grace.
Heavenly sounds were emitted
By each rotating, rectangular face.

Listening to it intensely,
I discovered a similarity

Between the different melodies
Rising from the tiny cavities
Of its various sides.
They sounded like twin melodies,
Conversing with each other,
Like dialogues,
Consisting of questions and answers,
Between sisters and brothers.

The music suddenly ended and the angel wanted to make sure that I had paid attention and understood the strange, unique structure of the short composition I had just heard. So, she started questioning and instructing me.

Listen and come closer.
Did you notice a similarity
Between the melody
I just played for thee
And the music of Bach,
Your favorite composer?
Did it remind you
Of his variations on a theme?
The composition so often you heard
In your waking state
And in your dream?

You can relate
To its points and counterpoints

By considering them twin notes
Connected at their joints.
We have respect and admiration
For Johann Sebastian Bach.
He is an inspiration
And a saintly revelation
To the great musicians
At Heaven's artistic station.
Before we leave
We wanted to give you
All that information.

I couldn't believe my eyes and ears. She went on and on, instructing me about the magical world of music. As I was listening, I felt joy within me growing and growing, and such a peacefulness descended upon me. Yet, as time went on, I became uneasy again. There was a problem which was still bothering me. I was searching for an answer to an important question which I had carried in my mind for some time. I knew that if anyone could answer my question, it would be an angel sent from Heaven, being knowledgeable in the domain of the spirit. But it was such a personal question, that I didn't want my daughter to hear it.

So I said, "I'd like to ask you a personal question. This question is so personal that I want to whisper it in your ear."

She said, "Okay, bring your lips close to my ear. I am listening."

My daughter was so curious, she said, "Mother, why can't I listen too?"

"No, this is something very personal."

I put my lips close to the ear of the angel. My daughter tried to come close to listen in.

The angel pointed a finger at her and said, "No, no, this is a secret to be respected."

I asked the angel, "Tell me, please, is there any true love on Earth? I've had disappointment in love. I wonder if genuine true love exists?"

The angel asked me, "Did you hear our melody?"

I replied, "Yes, yes, of course."

She said, "Do you know what it is called? I'll tell you a secret." Then she whispered in my ear, "This is the Song of Love. If love didn't exist, how could a beautiful melody like that be born, and how could this melody warm your heart? Didn't it warm your heart?"

"Yes, yes," I was whispering.

She stated, "Didn't it bring you joy and fulfillment? Didn't you feel that a cloud was lifted from your soul?"

I acknowledged her statement. "Yes, yes, it's true, it's true!"

She said, "If that is true, then love lives within you and also around you. Listen to its haunting melody! Then you will feel the love and understand its true nature."

Then, the angels picked up their flutes and a heavenly melody resounded in the air. I listened and listened to it, and my heart rejoiced. Such happiness and calm descended upon me. I wished that I could sing this melody to myself, that I could try to remember it. I wanted to remember each and every note. And, if I could remember them, then I could maybe carve my own magic flute. I believe in miracles, and I could then play my own Song of Love.

Suddenly, everything disappeared. I opened my eyes, wondering where I was. I realized that I must have been in the same place all along, in our bed, lying next to my husband. My head was resting on his chest. I felt his warm embrace and the happiness of love.

I whispered to myself, "Yes, yes, love is not only in Heaven, but love exists on Earth, too."

The angel was right. There was love within my heart and there was love coming from the pulsating melody of my husband's heartbeat. Our two hearts' synchronized beatings gave birth to my newborn Song of Love.

Song of Love

In the Magic Garden of Lust
High above the earth's solid crust,
Guardian angels hover above
The Sacred Paradise of Love.
They sustain the Flames of Passion
And protect the pearls of True Affection.
That is the place where we belong,
Far away from the earthly throng.

Come with me and you will see
The enchanting face of Eternity.
Let us yield our hearts to pleasure,
Let us shield Amour's Great Treasure,
Let us pray to be allowed to stay
And not be chased away
From that blessed place,
Filled with such beauty and grace.
Let us ask that we never be forced to leave
Like those two sinners, Adam and Eve.

God will listen to our plea
And not inflict upon us any penalty,
If we make very sure
That our love is sincere and pure.
Almighty is patient, tolerant,
And kind to those
Who are spiritually close,
Whose love is not shattered
By the hard rocks of time,
Whose deeds are not stained
By dirt and grime,
Who are one in body and soul,
Who select honesty as their highest goal,
Who are not guided by jealousy,
Whose hearts are free
From greed and conceit
And exempt from deceit,
Who are not carried away by emotion,
Who practice discipline, loyalty, devotion,

Compassion and tolerance.
Those who comply
With these rules of acceptance
Will win the grand price of admittance
To Love's Sacred Paradise.
The Creator knows that genuine love
Of a special kind
Is hard to find.
Therefore, all the submissions
Are carefully analyzed
Before being finalized.
The admissions are reserved for only a few
Loving couples like me and you.

Our total commitment to each other
From now on, forever,
And our tight embrace
Will touch the heart
Of each ethereal, heavenly grace.
We will be happy and proud
To be in the company
Of the celestial crowd.
Only true affection
Can evoke God's help, approval,
And protection,
Lifting us upwards,
Into the right direction.

Ten years later, on June 17, 1991,
the three angels returned.

The Magic Flute

Three angels from Heaven
Were sent to me,
Clad in the transparent veil
Of innocence and purity.
A golden halo was glowing
Above each saintly head.
One of them said:

We are your comforting friends.
In order to reach you
We flew over many strange lands.
We possess the foresight of oracles
And the power of miracles.
We can't stay here for very long,
Our mission is to play for you a song,
The title of which
Is not to be revealed,
Until your injured heart is healed.

Motionless I stood
In front of the three Graces,
Kindness was reflected

On their gentle faces.
Each one was holding a magic flute.
When the small, simple instruments
Carved from virgin wood touched their lips,
A melody of exquisite beauty
And great intensity
Hit my ears,
Chasing away my anguish,
Stopping my tears.

The celestial music filtered its way
Into my soul and body,
Melting slowly my frozen heart.
At the beginning,
Drops of joy were dripping,
Then, the ice of sadness cracked,
The dam of doom collapsed,
Torrents of happiness were gushing down,
Giving birth to
Swelling rivers of ecstasy.
My spirit was floating
In the strong currents of reverie.
The three angels were hovering over me.

Suddenly my miraculous trance ended.
To my surprise,
My body in space was suspended,
And in my hand a magic flute landed.
The angels were at my side
Securing my glide.

Together we slowly descended.
Miraculously, in my bedroom
We softly landed.
Before me were standing
The three Graces,
And a big smile ran across
Their joyful faces.
I was stunned with consternation,
And swept by a feeling of unearthly elation,
I burst into a loud exclamation:

"God's sacred messengers,
Heaven's miracle workers,
Thank you for bestowing upon me
Such peace and serenity!
Your glorious tune
Dispelled my doom,
Changed my dark mood,
Restored my livelihood,
And cured my heart.
Tell me, please, before we part,
The title of your melody."

Dear friend,
The magic flute in your hand
Will answer this question.
Keep it in your sight
Day and night.
It is a unique gift

Which is brand new,
Designed in Heaven especially for you,
To give your low spirit a lift.
Within its hollow cavity
A message you will find,
A secret for you left behind.
Soon we will have to go.

"No! No! Please stay a little longer
Until I feel much stronger.
Besides, I am just a terrestrial.
How can I play this celestial instrument?
Please give me a clue!"

Before we depart,
We will explain
How it works for you.
Although we've reached the limit
Of our short terrestrial visit,
Your wish will be granted.

We will fulfill our sacred task,
By answering some of the questions
You may want to ask.

"May I have a close look
At your magic flutes? "

There is no time for that anymore,
Our stay on Earth,
As we mentioned before,
Is limited.
We gave you a magic flute,
Which was made in Heaven,
Just like ours.
Creating it took many hours!
Place your flute before your eyes.
Even in Paradise
There are very few
Of the kind we bestowed upon you.
We will teach you to play
But with you, we can't stay.
So, you have to learn fast!
Try to do your best
And pass all the required tests,
While our visit lasts.

"Tell me please,
Why is this magic instrument,
This precious present
Of the firmament,
Rectangular and not round like ours? "

Because it is somewhat different
From the ones we use
On our earthly tours.

It has a special construction.
Don't pay too much attention to its exterior,
It is only a hard shell.
But, within its interior,
Many complex musical notes dwell.
They will feed on your breath,
They will grow from your lips.
Before we leave,
We will give you some helpful tips.

"Please clarify,
Why is each square side
Equipped with so many holes?"

These are the openings
Through which music rolls,
Containing many wondrous notes.
If you listen to these carefully,
You will hear a sea of melody.

"Forgive me for my curiosity,
But how can a modest musical instrument
Hold within its cavity
Such a variety of sounds
And pleasing notes?"

Because it has secret symbols and codes.
This magic flute has four sides.

It is really bigger than it seems,
It is equipped with many tiny holes
And shining beams.
It holds the light and the air of the sky.
Take it in your hands,
Don't be shy.
Each note that you hear
Has many groups of sounds.
Draw these near,
And magical bars of music will appear.
We will teach you how to play,
But with you we cannot stay,
So, you have to learn it fast!
Try to do your best,
While our visit lasts.

"My saviors, before you go,
A very personal question I would like to ask."

The Angel of Wisdom will be the best
To fulfill that task.

"Angel of Wisdom,
I want to whisper in your ear.
Please, tell me,
Where is true love?
Is it far, nowhere, or near?"

Your magic flute has the answer.
We came for a special purpose,
Our task is accomplished.
It's time for us to leave.
Now, you are on your own.
Relax your forehead,
Don't wear worry's frown.
We leave you this sheet of instructions,
Read it carefully
And you cannot fail.
Be strong, hopeful, courageous,
Not weak and frail.
You will see and feel love
At your side.
Follow the instructions in this guide.

Please understand
That we must leave this land.
Goodbye, our dear friend.
We fulfilled our earthly task,
Don't ask us to stay any longer.
Accept with grace
That we must abandon this place.
Before we go on our way,
For you we want to pray.
Pick up your flute, be gentle and kind,
Study the score we leave behind,

Look at the musical bars.
On your flute you will find
Drawings of the moon and the stars,
Etched with finesse on the virgin wood,
By the great masters of the sky.

Before we say our final goodbye,
We want to tell you,
That we register love in Heaven each day.
Be patient, don't get discouraged,
Don't run away.
Pick up your flute and play!
You know in your heart
The music and the words you want to say.
Say it loud, you know to whom,
The one who 45 years ago
Was your bridegroom.
Since then, he is your loving husband
With whom you share all these years,
Your joy and tears.

Today is his birthday,
We leave a special gift for him too,
Along with a blank card,
To be filled out only by you.
Take these dozen magic red roses,
They will perform miracles for both of you.

The words you will write on the card
Have to be sincere and true!
Otherwise, the roses will disappear,
And only an ugly, empty, grey,
Dull vase will appear.

"But why isn't the card signed
By all of you?"

Because you are the one to carry on
With our teachings and advice.
You are the one to guess and to discover
The secret magical power
Of love and happiness,
And the title of our song.
To this planet you belong.
We are just the delegates
Of the celestial throng,
Sent to help and to guide.
We will be always at your side.
Now is the time
To draw your lips
To your magic flute.
We gave you all
The necessary tips
To sing a heavenly song.
We know you can do it,
We are never wrong!

Inhale the sweet fragrance
Of the celestial roses.
Admire their great beauty,
And a great feeling of love
Will descend upon thee.

Now pick up our card
And concentrate hard.
Be careful what you write!
Before we go out of sight,
We have to make sure
That all your words are right,
And your thoughts are honest and pure.
Therefore, to your conscience we appeal.
Only then can we conclude
Our sacred deal,
And apply upon your written note
Our celestial seal,
In order to verify
That you wrote the truth
And not a lie.
We must comply
To this prescribed rule of the sky.
We can't leave Earth,
Nor greet the rising sun,
Before this deed is done.

I picked up a pen
From my nearby den,
And I completed promptly,
The blank card given to me:

To My Dear Husband

Three angels from Heaven
Came to me today,
Bringing these magic red roses
For your birthday.
There are no traces
Of blemishes
On these velvety, soft faces.
These magnificent perfect flowers
Bloom each day, high above.
They display their beauty
In the Paradise of Love.
They are imbibed and blessed
With a delightful heavenly scent.
Their delivery is a sacred event.
They contain in their delicate fragrance
The essence of love's magical potion,
Which evokes in us when inhaled,
Feelings of deep affection,
And great devotion.

I was told that they belong
To you and me,
Because our love is constant and strong,
Honest and pure.
Therefore, this card holds
The celestial signature . . .
But it is written and signed by me,
Your loving wife,
Whose heart is committed to you
Till death will us part!

A glowing golden seal
On my completed card appeared,
But the angels disappeared
And the magic flute vanished from my hand.

I was in our bedroom,
Lying next to my husband.
There were a dozen red roses in full bloom
Along with a large card,
Placed on our nightstand.
Their sweet intoxicating fragrance
Filled the air,
I wondered how they got there.
I couldn't tell,
There was no one anywhere,
I was still under the angels' spell.

My head was resting on my husband's chest,
My heart was pounding in my breast,

I felt his arm around my shoulder
And I knew that I belonged to him forever.
Being closed in his embrace
Was so divine,
His warm breath touched mine.
I gently kissed his face,
My pulse started to race.
I closed my eyes,
Feeling high up in space,
In Heaven's Paradise,
The place where passion never dies,
Where our genuine love for each other
Will never wither,
Or fade away.
It will bloom each day
Like magic roses.
It will never lose its beauty,
Neither its enchanting quality,
Or its freshness.
It will stay locked in our hearts forever,
Bringing us joy, contentment and happiness.

The rhythmic sound
Of my beloved's heartbeat
And the pulsating rhythm
Of my own heart,
Setting the speed and harmony,
Brought me back to reality.
I sensed such joy and ecstasy!

My eyes searched for the magic flute
But it was nowhere.
Yet, I could hear a melody
Of exquisite beauty,
Played by invisible hands
Around me.
Someone I couldn't see
Was speaking to me:

By now we think
You are ready
To guess the title of our melody,
The one we played previously
For thee.

"It is the Song of Love," I said.
The music stopped abruptly after that,
But a different tune
Slowly filtered into my room.
Only a solo flute was playing
A song of great beauty,
And someone invisible was reciting
A poem called, "Peace, Joy and Serenity."
It was so strange,
Because I recognized my voice
And the melody of my choice.

I knew then the angels
And the magic flute

Were still with me.
I also realized
That true love is sublime.
Its passionate breath
Can activate my flute anytime,
Creating together my music and rhyme.
I also understood,
That there was no need for me
To sulk or to brood,
Because my true love will always be
At my side, at any age!
I learned the truth,
That affection and passion
Does not belong only to youth,
But they live and flourish
At life's every stage.

I also discovered the angels' assigned role,
Their main goal,
And the secret left behind.
Out of two loving heartbeats
Pulsating for each other,
The magic flute divined
The Song of Love—
But it was my composition,
My creation, born out of love
And imagination,
With Heaven's participation.

I knew that the magic flute
And the magic roses
Will always be
In my custody,
And help me to create
My songs of love,
With the help of Almighty
And the angels above.
Love, music and verse
Will never die
Because they are a part
Of the vast Universe,
And precious gifts
Sent to us from the sky.

Song of Love II

There is a Paradise on Earth
Where love gives birth
To happiness and joy …
Where angels fly above and cheer,
Where the sky is bright and clear …
Where white doves of peace appear,
Where sweet heavenly songs are born …
Where Cupid blows his magic horn
And throws his arrows
Of flaming passion
And deep affection
In every possible direction …

Dreamworld

Where gentleness and kindness dwell,
Where you succumb to a magical spell …
Where you seek and find
Contentment and peace of mind …
Where you can turn in your hour of doom
From the confinement of your room,
And leave behind your bitter tears
And all the heartaches of past years …

Where clinging to your lover's heart,
A wondrous journey you will start,
On the wings of ecstasy
And in the arms of reverie …
During your ecstatic ascent,
You will inhale passion's intoxicating scent …
When you reach Amour's Holy Land,
With your beloved, hand-in-hand,
You will understand
That love is a Sacred Covenant
And a precious gift
Of the distant firmament …
Then you will sing the Song of Love
With the angels from above.

Mystery

Somewhere, at the edge of nowhere,
Upon the unpaved road of the future,
The silhouette of my fate is projected ...
But my mortal eyes can't see
The shape of my destiny,
Nor can my spirit grasp
Life's unpredictable course of action ...
Only my striving body
Feels the agony of pain
And the joy of resurrection ...
I am but a wave
In the ocean of existence,
Driven by the current of my thoughts
And protected by God's assistance ...

How could I ever foresee what Fate had in store for me? I couldn't prevent being thrown forcefully into the Prison of Destiny. No words can express accurately the terrible feeling of losing my liberty.

One day I found myself locked in a room with no furniture in it whatsoever. Not even a bed to sleep on was provided; only the four white walls were surrounding me. I could see a rough, wooden floor and two slightly open windows reinforced with thick, massive iron bars. It looked like a prison from which there was no way to escape. I had no recollection of how I got there, and I felt desperate and helpless. Being highly agitated, I was pacing back and forth on the wooden floor trying to figure out what to do.

As I looked up towards the ceiling of my prison, I could see a horrifying, giant black spider slowly descending from one of the upper corners and staring at me with almost human-looking eyes and expression. I sensed that its intention was to stab me with its deadly poison.

I was terrified realizing that it was just a matter of time before the fatal bite would take place. I rushed to the window trying to see if I could somehow get away, but it was hopeless. There was not enough open space between the heavy iron bars to escape.

Through the partially open windows I could hear voices outside, but I couldn't see anyone around. The voices were loud and clear. It sounded like a chorus performing a merry, cheerful song. I could discern clearly each word of the lyrics behind the melody:

We are the divine Spirits of Freedom
And the children of Wisdom.
We are happy,
Joyful and carefree,
Living in Heaven's Kingdom.
Prisoner of Destiny,
Locked in your room,
In the Prison of Doom,
Take heart, don't fall apart,
Don't lose your hope!
Try to cope
With your pain and agony.

Someday you will be set free
And sing with us
The Song of Liberty.

While the singing was going on, I could see to my amazement the Statue of Liberty walking by my window and looking in. I cried out, "Mother of Exiles, please set me free! You are the symbol of Freedom! Please give me shelter. Help me to get away from this prison where I was placed unjustly." But the Statue of Liberty looked at me and silently passed by. I couldn't understand the indifference she manifested towards me.

Then I remembered that she was just a statue, only a symbol. Her heart didn't beat the pulse of life. Yet I wanted to believe that she could still help me in a mysterious, spiritual way. After she walked away I was disappointed, discouraged, and terrified. As I looked up again I could see the black spider descending further and further down on the wall. This time it seemed somewhat faster than before, heading towards me.

At this point I ran to the entrance door of my cell, but there was no way I could open it. I didn't have a key. I was frantically banging and pushing the door, time and time again, until finally to my surprise it opened.

There was a concrete driveway in front of me leading to a broad street. I perceived a black carriage drawn by two black horses, driven by a driver dressed in black and wearing a tall black hat. A coffin was placed inside the carriage. I could see it through the sliding-glass door facing me. I realized with horror that it was a horse-drawn hearse carrying the dead, one of the many I had seen a long time ago in the city where I grew up.

What a sinister sight. It gave me the shivers. The hearse stopped at the entrance to the driveway.

The driver descended from his seat and came towards me. He tipped his hat and addressed me! He seemed to be well mannered and courteous.

"I came to liberate you from your captivity and from your emotional pain and suffering. I will take you from here in my distinguished black carriage reserved for special occasions!"

"It looks to me like you are headed for a funeral service. Who is the person whom you are carrying in the coffin for the last rites?"

"Would you like me to show you?"

"No, I don't want to see the face of any dead person. It will give me nightmares. It isn't important to me anyway. Probably it is someone whom I had never met. Can I join you on the driver's seat? I must get out of this place. It is life threatening to me. It would be a very kind gesture on your part to give me a ride."

"Not before I reveal to you who is in the coffin. Come and look!"

The driver pushed aside the glass door surrounding the coffin and lifted the lid. But there was no sign of a body inside.

"How come you are carrying an empty coffin? Are you on your way to pick up the corpse from the funeral parlor? You can drop me off on your way. It would be very helpful to me. I would be very grateful to you for your assistance."

"Can't you guess who I am and my destination?"

"Who are you? I never met you before."

"I am Death. This coffin was reserved for you to take you out of your misery. You asked for freedom. I am here to give it to you."

"I don't deserve the freedom you offer. I am not ready yet to leave this earth. I have too many goals to fulfill. Besides, I am not old enough to part with life. Under these circumstances your help is not welcome. I will try to help myself somehow the best I can. Hope hasn't left me yet."

"You must understand that I never tolerate disobedience, disapproval, nor criticism from anybody. I can show up any time unexpectedly and extinguish the flame of life."

"I am the ultimate fate of man.
You may resist and fight me
As long as you can,
But the final outcome
Will always be the same.
I am the winner in life's game."

"Not quite!
You have no control
Over the soul
And its sacred sanctuary.
The spirit is free,
Defying you and finality."

"I am not interested in your personal philosophy. You will find out the truth by coming with me."

"Please have mercy! Let me live at least for a few more years."

"I am not compassionate. No one can control my actions and my desires. You should know that only I can liberate you from your prison. That is what you wanted and now you are going to get it my way."

Death was about to grab me and I knew that his intention was to put me in the coffin and take me away in the ultimate, eternally sealed prison from which I could never escape. It would be the end of me.

I was determined to escape from Death's grip somehow, someway.

Suddenly, I was possessed by a powerful great force that was brought on by my fierce desire to live. I was running down the driveway at the speed of lightening it seemed, towards the entrance of my prison room. I felt that it would be safer there inside than to stay with Death outside. But Death was following me.

Nevertheless, miraculously I managed to get inside at the last moment. Fortunately the door was open when I reached it.

As soon as I entered into my prison room, the entrance door was locked behind me by invisible hands.

For some strange reason Death couldn't pass through it. I was pleased that I was out of his reach.

Safe and secure inside, I heard the carriage being driven away. It was such a relief. But just when I was feeling so much better being out of danger, the black spider appeared in front of me.

Untitled Story

Foreword

Dear readers of my poetry,
I will relate to you the true story
Of a bizarre incident
Which happened to me.
Although, it took place many years ago,
It is still fresh in my memory.
In my writing I convey,
The dreadful event I experienced
On a particular day
In the month of May.
Please be attentive and receptive
To my following poetic narrative.
I must mention
And bring to your attention,
That at the time
This weird happening occurred,
I was somewhat confused and perturbed,
By being under the spell
Of the strange creative spirits
Which in my soul dwell.
Therefore, I can't tell
Whether my mysterious encounter
Was real, supernatural, or fictitious.

I also have great difficulty
In giving the right title
To my mystical story.
What should I call
This fantastic occurrence?
Should I name it:
Escape and Deliverance?
The Face of Reality?
The Tricks of Destiny?
Or, The Price We Pay for Curiosity?
I have to state
That until this date,
I haven't ceased to contemplate,
Which one of these titles listed above
Would be most appropriate
To my odd tale.
But, still I fail
To reach any conclusion.
I can't overcome my indecision.

So, my dear readers,
Listen to my plea.
Study carefully
The text of my poetry,
And please find for me
The best title to my sinister story.

Untitled Story

It was a beautiful day
At the end of May.
I was strolling along the countryside,
Looking for a secluded, quiet place
Where I could hide.
I was treading for hours
The earth's green face,
Watching the blooming flowers,
Listening to the twitter of the birds
Perched on the tall trees,
Loaded with fresh new leaves,
And to the sound of the crickets
As they were hopping around
On the grass-covered ground.
Colorful butterflies were flapping
Their dainty wings in the air
With such ease and flair.

After awhile, I got tired of walking.
I was ready for settling somewhere
In a remote, peaceful corner.
Eventually I came across
An isolated, solitary nook
Located near a gently flowing brook.
Deciding not to go any further,
I sat down next to the clear water,
And looked up to the blue sky,

With no trace of clouds passing by.
I was enjoying the warm sun,
All my previous anxieties and worries were gone.

Suddenly, I heard the sound of thunder.
It was so strange,
Because the weather didn't seem to change.
I couldn't explain what was happening and why,
As I was sitting under a cloudless sky.
There were no evident indications
Of any approaching storm or rain.
But, the disquieting detonations
And electrical explosions
Came closer and closer
To where I was resting.
They were becoming more and more frightening,
Annoying and distressing.

Then, my eyes fell
Upon a reckless rider,
Looking like a strange apparition
Rising from Hell,
And heading in my direction,
Disturbing the peace and serenity
Of the beautiful season of spring.
With his whip, he was striking constantly.
His fast, galloping horse.
The black stallion
Followed his master's wild course,
Without rebellion.

I felt outraged at the sight
Of such cruelty.
So, I called out loudly,
Addressing the unruly and fiery jockey,
Trying to reason and communicate
With that rough, faithless apostate:

"Slow down, whoever you are!
If you keep up like that
You will not get too far!
Why are you so dismal
To your devoted, loyal animal?
Why do you force him
To comply to your sickly whim?
Are you a monstrous person
Of a special kind?
An aberration of some sort
Of mankind?
Please heed my advice,
Be reasonable and wise.
Ride more carefully
And don't treat your black stallion,
Your devoted companion, so badly."

It seemed that the racing jockey
Heard my plea,
Because he slowed down gradually,
Leading his horse steadily,
In a continuous slow-moving pace,
Towards my resting place.

Then ultimately,
He stopped in front of me.

He wore a white mask on his face,
His body was wrapped in a black sheet,
I couldn't detect even his feet.
He stood motionless and silent,
At that point he didn't look mean or violent.

I couldn't control my curiosity,
I wanted to find out, who is he?
So I started talking to him
Without interruption,
Carried away by anger, dismay,
And compassion.

"Who are you, mysterious stranger?
What is compelling you
To ignore kindness and danger?
Where do you lead your dedicated steed
With such force and speed?

"With what kind of special, poisonous potion
Do you feed your valiant, strong horse,
To be so fast and fiery,
Coercing him to follow willingly and blindly
Your assigned treacherous course?
And what harmful, bewitching mixture
Do you administer
To your faithful, wild creature,

In order to alter
His true innate rebellious, defiant proud nature,
Rendering him submissive,
Compliant, patient and tolerant
To your crude, insensitive treatment?

"But, I can foresee
That someday
You will pay dearly
For your irresponsibility,
Inconsideration, carelessness and cruelty,
When your wild stallion
Will start his rebellion
Against your torture and tyranny.
Then, he will defy your command
And he will not tolerate anymore
Your torment and harsh treatment.
He will not cater to your desire.
When his patience and tolerance will expire,
He will release his repressed anger and rage
From their locked cage,
And he will set them on fire.

Then your obedient, abused, exploited slave
Will become again rebellious, defiant and brave.
He will break his harness,
Fighting fiercely for his freedom and happiness.
He will throw you to the ground,
He will trample on you
And he will kick you around.

After his deed of revenge will be done,
He will jump and run,
Regaining his lost courage and pride.
And he will not mind leaving you behind,
Bleeding to death by the wayside.
Therefore, if you don't want to die,
To the rules of discipline you must comply."

The weird jockey
Broke his silence finally
And began talking to me:

I don't have patience for you anymore,
You are going to get
What you are not looking for.
I have something shocking for you in store!
I listened long enough
To your senseless, dull, lengthy monologue.
Now, it is your turn to pay attention
To my prologue:

I am the representative
Of sickness and decay.
You will curse incessantly the day
On which you met me.
I create terror, horror, and fear
Wherever I appear.
I can open any door
And perform inside anyplace,
My ugly, awesome chore.
I can tease, torture and harass

Wherever I pass through,
And meet defenseless, weak, insolent,
Arrogant and conceited people like you.

I can intimidate, humiliate
And subdue anyone
Whenever I want to,
Deriving from it pleasure and fun.
I rejoice when I see someone
In great suffering and agony,
So, beware of me!
No one can anticipate
My sudden appearance,
I am a threat to existence.

Nobody can prevent me
From carrying out my mission,
Consisting of life's execution.
I am someone you can't love,
But you can hate,
I am the executive delegate of fate.
You will respect me,
When I reveal to you
My face and body,
And you will also realize
That accosting me was not wise!
You will see what a high price you will pay
For your uncontrolled curiosity.

At that point the mysterious jockey
Removed his mask from his face

And the black sheet from his body.
My heart almost stopped its beat,
Because all I could see
Was a bare skull, naked bones
And two black holes,
In the place where the eyes are supposed to be.
He was addressing me
With a hoarse and coarse voice:

To stop here was not my choice.
By now, I suppose you know my name
And the purpose of my game.
As you probably noticed,
My voice is rough and deep.
I am the vendor of eternal sleep,
And the nightmare of everybody.
No one can make fun of me!
Listen, mortal stranger,
Beware of my revenge and anger.
I have a violent temper!
Be courteous, humble and polite,
Otherwise, I might strike you
With my invisible scythe,
Bringing upon you the curse of blight.
I always carry with me my useful tool,
Nobody can take me for a fool!

The ghastly specter,
The vile demolisher,
Seemed pleased and amused

To see me utterly astonished and confused,
Trembling like a dying leaf,
Stricken by fright and grief.
He continued his threatening speech
Without inhibition,
With no intermission:

Who do you think you are
To allow yourself to go so far
As to criticize, to judge or to analyze
My conduct or action?
You better apologize!
Or, you are in for a big surprise!
I have a tendency to tantalize
And to kill with my sharp device.
My touch is as cold as ice!
All over the world I roam,
And everywhere I feel at home.
I travel constantly
From the North to the South Pole,
Fulfilling my sole mission and goal:
The destruction of the body and soul.
I am known to be heartless and evil,
I am compared to the Devil.

I was speechless and terrified,
I felt helpless, terrorized and victimized
By that undesirable predator,
Whose intention seemed to be
To monitor my heartbeat

And to put me
To eternal sleep.
I knew that I had made a grave mistake,
And due to that, my life was at stake.

I was asking desperately
That ruthless manifestation of horror,
That brutal molester,
To forgive me,
Addressing him with humility:

"Powerful Shadow,
I stand in awe before you.
What can I say or do
To make peace with you?
Please, don't take me away,
Don't use me as your prey!
I am willing to repent,
Be merciful and tolerant."

But the gruesome apparition
Had no favorable reaction
To my fervent plea.
He didn't show any sign of pity.
On the contrary,
He continued to threaten me
Even more vehemently:

I ignore your appeal!
You can't make with Death

Any special deal,
Or escape his wrath.
I don't believe in mercy or concession,
I have no compassion,
I detest forgiveness and protection,
I don't make any exception!
Neither do I have tolerance
For disrespect and arrogance.
You will suffer for your offense.
You deeply hurt my pride,
And interrupted my ride.
Therefore, I will not step aside!
With you I will stay.
You can't get away
Without my severe punishment.
You will not escape
My harsh treatment.

Now that I am here,
It should be very clear,
That you might have to come with me,
Regardless to what degree
You despise my company,
And experience my adventurous,
Perilous, and foreboding journey.
You have become the victim
Of your curiosity.

I was begging despondently
My loathsome persecutor,

My abominable tormentor,
For understanding and sympathy:

"Please don't take me along!
It would be so wrong and unfair,
Because I have to take care of my family—
They will be brokenhearted and lost without me.
Besides, I love my life
And I would like to continue my strife,
Regardless how difficult it may be.
I want to be healthy, safe and sound
Going happily around.

"I have lots of goals to fulfill,
I am not ready yet
To pay life's final bill.
Therefore, please, allow me
To jump over that nearby fence
And don't take my request as an offense,
But merely as a self-defense,
In order to get out of your way.
I would like to stay
On that other side,
And behind those tall, distant bushes
I would like to hide,
Giving you ample free space
For your fast ride."

Then, the horrid specter of oblivion
Expressed his opinion:

Courageous mortal is your name,
You attained power and fame,
Yet you tremble before me,
Refusing my company.
Although you act like a coward,
You still deserve an award from me,
Because I have to admit
That despite your character deficit,
I must give you credit
For daring to stop and to affront Death.
So, I present to you
My precious, concealed open casket
Filled with foul, expired human breath.

The ruthless, cruel specter
Forced me to inhale
The poisonous, stale exhalations,
Which gave me mortifying hallucinations.
They were terrible visions
Of myself being pushed
Into Death's empty coffin
And taken for a dangerous ride,
Then being buried alive.
In my insane delusion
And total confusion,
I kicked the tightly closed lid of the coffin
And kept yelling:

"This can't be true!
This can't be true! "

But, nobody was coming to my rescue.
I was choking and suffocating,
I felt that I was dying.
I started screaming and crying:

"A terrible injustice was done,
I was proclaimed dead,
But, I am not really gone!
I want to come out and see the Sun."

After awhile I realized
That my lamentations
And my desperate cry
Were senseless and futile,
Because there was nobody around
Above the ground
Who could save me,
And not let me die.
I was hopeless and powerless
Locked in my solitary underground,
Where there was no movement, no sound.
There was no chance for salvation,
I knew that I was gradually approaching
Life's final station,
Feeling devastated and extremely weak.
My vision was blurred,
And I couldn't speak.
As I was fighting fiercely
For each breath
In my dark grave,

I could hear clearly
The powerful, sinister voice of Death,
Resounding in my sealed cave:

*Struggling mortal,
You will soon enter my black portal.
Heed my words:
I am the absolute ruler
Beneath the earth.
Your ultimate fate
Was planned at your birth.
No amount of awe and sorrow
Can change your destiny.
From now on forever
You belong to me!
Nobody can ever touch my acquired property.
Accept bravely your suffering and pain,
Your effort to survive is in vain.
You will eternally remain
In my cold, dreary and unfriendly domain.*

Then suddenly I came back to reality.
In a state of agony and despair,
I was still gasping for air.
The cruel torturer was at my side
Robbing totally my confidence and pride.
He resumed his malicious, sleek rhetoric,
Disregarding my suffering and panic:

I can't stop laughing and rejoicing,

While you are coughing and choking.
But relax, don't despair,
Soon you will again get fresh air.
I will release you from my spell
And you will get well,
Because this time I leave you behind.
Once in awhile,
I am merciful and kind.
Besides, you are not yet listed in my file.
But, I couldn't resist
Showing you the extent of my power
By giving you a sample
Of what it would be like,
The agonizing plight of your last hour!

But, it is such a shame
That I can't stay any longer
And play with you over and over,
My funny, enjoyable game!
It was amusing and pleasurable to witness
Your physical and mental distress.
I would derive lots of satisfaction
Even from a single additional repetition
Of my previous action.

But my time is up
And I have to go on
To my next stop,
Looking forward to some more fun.
I have an important appointment to keep,

With someone, whom I must put to eternal sleep.
But, remember, mortal stranger,
That someday I will be back!
And then, your life will be in great danger,
Because I will force you to ride with me
On the back of my fast, galloping horse,
Exposing your soul and body
To my dangerous, bumpy and devious course!
I will have no sympathy or consideration
For your emotional frustration and strain,
Nor for your discomfort and pain.

I also have in mind
To subject you in the future
To a special kind of torture,
By bringing upon you
A terrible affliction
Of a specific nature.
But, it will not be the outgrowth
Of fantasy and fiction.

There will be no more spells induced by me,
No tricks of imagination,
No illusionary visions and impressions.
You will suffer in silence intensely
In the world of reality.
You will not exert any resistance,
On the contrary,
You will beg for my assistance,
Offering to give up voluntarily

Your cherished existence.
Then you will see
That I manifest occasionally
Understanding and mercy.
I will fulfill your desire
By helping you to expire.
You will experience
The painful and sorrowful sensation
Of your life's real and final cessation.

Death again put on his camouflage,
Disguising his body and visage,
And laughing heartily
He finally left me,
Riding wildly as before,
And disappearing into the nearby forest.
But, I couldn't rest peacefully anymore,
Nor could I enjoy
The beauty of the outdoor.
I was agitated, frightened and uneasy.
Death planted in me
The seeds of horror, terror and insanity.
I ran home frantically,
And bolted behind me quickly
The front door.
Standing on the entrance hall's tiled floor,
I listened intently,
Still not feeling safe inside,
Still troubled, shocked, confused, and terrified,
Thinking that maybe Death followed me from behind.

I was dazed, like in a trance,
Reflecting on my miraculous escape
And my magical deliverance.
Suddenly I realized
That my life is precious and dear,
And it became very clear
In my mind,
That the best way to find
Peace and serenity,
And to overcome fear and anxiety,
Was to pray to God everyday,
Asking Almighty
To keep Death from me away.
I broke into tears,
Beseeching the Creator to grant me
Many happy and healthy years.

Epilogue

Never insult Death.
Don't ever provoke his wrath,
Because he can still your breath.
If someday he happens to come your way,
Don't accost him,
But let him pass freely through,
Be happy and grateful
That he didn't come for you!

The Search for My True Self

Where are you, my true self?
Did you get lost in the maze of destiny?
Did the passing years
Snatch you away from me?
I remember when you were at my side.
We walked together the city streets
And the countryside.
We were always a good team
And now, you appear only in my dream.

Why did you leave me behind?
Why were you so selfish and unkind?
Wherever you are,
No matter how far,
Please come and join me
On my life's terrain.
I want to be with you again!
At one point on my earthly station
I went through a great transformation
And I noticed your absence,
I missed your presence.
You were always silent and reserved,
Content and undisturbed.
Did you ever miss my company?
You are a part of me,
My spiritual self.

Why do you ignore me
And place me on a shelf?
I hope to find you one day
And then, forever,
With me you will stay!

It was the night before my birthday. I tossed around for hours in my bed. I couldn't fall asleep no matter how hard I tried. All kinds of thoughts passed through my mind. I recalled the different episodes of my life. I evoked the times when I faced very difficult periods of my existence, when I had to cope with trying and emotionally painful experiences. I also reflected on the happy and pleasant times of my life.

Finally, after a long period of all these silent meditations, I did fall asleep and I had a very strange dream. In my dream I was looking for my true self. I had the feeling that my true self was somewhat lost. I was thinking that I was just one day away from my sixty-ninth birthday. The realization that my youth was gone made me sad. I felt that somewhere along the way I had lost my true self. Or perhaps my true self had gone through some transformations and I wanted to find out who this new person was.

The years can transform us, not to the point of becoming completely different people, but maybe we do become altered in many ways. Alterations take place through all the life experiences we encounter through the years. Various stages of our lives can perhaps kill something in us, but at the same time something new is born in its place. Parts of our old selves are affected and some of these parts are destroyed. In their place, new facets of our self get created.

In my dream, these were my thoughts as I walked on a familiar street. It was a cool, fall day. The leaves were turning and I could see some falling leaves blown by the wind. I was walking on that familiar street as though it were the street where I lived; yet it looked a little bit different than in my waking state. I had seen someone coming my way from a distance, and I recognized the person. It was my true self! She looked like a teenager, like me a long time ago when I was a young girl. She was approaching me and I felt such happiness. *Finally*, I was thinking, *I found my true self*, and as she came closer, we embraced each other. I said, "Oh, my God, my true self! I haven't seen you in such a long time. I'm so happy that you are here! Where were you all this time? I was looking for you."

"I was always with you."

"Why didn't I see you? You couldn't have been with me all this time."

"Yes, I was with you, I was there all along."

"How is it I didn't see you, I didn't hear you speak?"

"Because you were never listening to me. You were acting as though I were nonexistent."

"I can't believe you. This can't be true."

"You want me to prove it?" And suddenly, she disappeared.

"Oh no!, I finally found my true self, and now she's gone." I called out, "Where are you, my true self? Where did you go?"

I heard a voice within telling me, *I'm right here. I was always here, but you weren't aware of me. Or maybe you forgot about me*?

Then, suddenly there was a silence and gradually a dense fog was forming all around me. All the people in the street, and everything else, disappeared. I was so confused. I didn't know what to do or where to go. I couldn't see anything. I couldn't follow any direction. I cried out, "True Self, what's happening to me? What is this? Where am I? I'm scared. I'm surrounded by vapors."

My true self said, *You are shedding too many tears. These vapors are formed by the tears you shed.*

I asked, "What should I do?"

Suddenly, all the vapors disappeared and I heard my true self talking to me, *You have to get away from here in order to find your true self.*

"But you said you are always with me."

Then, she said, *Yes, still you have to get away from here. Run, run!*

"Why do I have to do that?"

Because you have to get acquainted with your true self. Your true self is like an alien to you. I want you to understand your true self, who you really are. And for that, you have to leave this place.

I started running desperately, thinking, *It is good that I can run so fast because I used to run marathons and now I can run long distances and get away fast from this place.*

I ran and ran, leaving the city behind. The fall landscape continued, there was also a cool wind. I was scared, but I knew I had to keep on running.

Then I came to a road that looked like a country road with no end. There were no buildings in sight. Having no sense of direction, I wondered where I was heading. I asked my true self, "True Self, speak up! You were complaining that I never listen to you, but I want to listen to you now. Tell me, where am I?"

My true self was silent. So I kept on running, and I came to a bifurcation. In my desperation I asked myself, "Now there are two roads here diverging; which should I take, the left or the right one?" Again I addressed my true self, "True self, speak up now!" My true self was silent. I told myself, "I'm going to pick one of the roads. I'm picking the one on the left." I ran and ran desperately and it led me to nowhere. After awhile I thought, *No, I have to turn back and take the road on the right.* So I ran all the way back to the bifurcation and followed the road on the right.

Again I ran and grew increasingly tired. The wind started blowing and I could see dried leaves on the ground. I could also perceive the rusty-colored grass. It was like a desert covered with grass and dried leaves. I wondered, *Where did the leaves come from? I don't even see trees.*

Suddenly, I detected a synagogue in the distance. As I came closer and closer, I noticed the Star of David on it. It was clear to me that this was a Jewish synagogue. The door was open and I entered. It seemed to me that there were people in the synagogue, and the thought came to my mind that I had come here to present a speech and read some of my poetry.

I walked up to the pulpit, began my speech, and then started reading my poetry. I got carried away and read on and on.

Suddenly, after quite awhile my eyes fell on the empty benches. There was no one in the synagogue. I was surprised and couldn't quite understand what was happening. *Why did I come here? Am I all right doing these things?* I looked around and felt confused and bewildered. I remembered that before I started talking, the sun was rising. Now, as I saw the synagogue door opening, the sun descended from the sky and entered into the synagogue!

I was even more surprised when the sun sat down in the first row of benches and started applauding. I thought, *Am I going insane? Am I hallucinating?*

The sun exclaimed, "Bravo, bravo!"

I said to the sun, "Tell me please, am I all right? Am I dreaming? There is no one here in this synagogue except for you. I have never seen the sun coming down from the sky. I never have heard of the sun talking. What's happening to me?"

The sun answered me to my great surprise. "Well, can you see anybody else here?"

"No, I can't see anyone."

"Is it possible there is someone here whom you can't see?"

"In my imagination it could only be a spirit. Who else but a ghost?"

"Did you ever think of God?"

"Oh, that's true … the spirit of God must be here. This is the house of God, the synagogue."

The sun asked me again, "But is there yet someone whom you can see? Look closely."

On the opposite side from where the sun was sitting, in the same row, there sat an angel. I asked myself, *Am I going insane?* I couldn't help getting panicky. I tried to talk to her, "Angel, what is happening to me? Am I going insane? Am I hallucinating? Am I seeing things that don't exist?"

The angel said, "No, you are all right."

"How come if I'm all right, I see such impossible things?"

"My child, these things are not impossible, because you are living in two worlds—the external world, and the internal, spiritual world. And both of these worlds are real—the world of reality and the world of fantasy. You can create different worlds in your imagination, but these are the creations of your mind. So you have created all these fantasies which look very real to you. Don't you have a world of reveries when you are asleep and you have dreams? That's your dreamworld and those dreams seem so real. In your dreams you can't even discern between fantasy and reality."

The angel continued asking me questions. "Just look closely. Do you see someone here? Someone sitting right here in the synagogue, waiting to be observed?"

As I looked between the angel and the sun, I could see my father sitting! He died long ago in the extermination camps of Dachau during the Holocaust. I realized that his spirit was there. But although it must have been only his spirit, he looked so real. He looked as he had long ago when I was a teenager. He died way back in 1944. So many years had passed by since then, but he looked the same, as young as when he was separated from me in the concentration camps of Auschwitz during World War II, when we were taken there as prisoners. I looked at my father and I said, "Oh, how come you are here? I haven't seen you for so long."

My father answered, “I came because I knew that you needed me.”

“I'm so glad that you came! Indeed, I need you! I had so many difficulties I had to go through. But I remember a time long ago when in my dreams I was looking for you. At that time also I had some difficulties to overcome. Do you remember? We met in my dreams.

“It was a long time ago, but I never forgot my dream. I was looking for you and I knew that you were in a building, which had several stories. As I entered it, I realized how many floors and doors it had. I figured that you must be in one of the rooms in that building. I checked all the doors on the first and second levels and they were all locked. Then, I ran up on the third floor and checked all the doors but they were also locked, except for one. I put my hand on that doorknob and turned it. The door opened. It was odd to find a room with no furniture, except in the middle of the room there was a big box. It wasn't just a box, it was a coffin. I felt you were inside. I banged my fists on the lid of the coffin, crying out, ‘Please, Father, I need you! Listen to me! Open up! Open up!’ But I understood that you coudn't open the coffin.

“At the same time, I felt that it would be a sacrilege to violate your final resting place. Still, I wanted to see you and talk to you. In my desperation, I tried to forcefully lift the lid of the coffin. Eventually, I was able to push up the lid. There you were, lying on your back motionless. Your eyes were closed. I talked to you. ‘Father! Father! Please wake up! I haven’t seen you for so long and I have so many things to tell you.’ But there was silence; you didn't answer. I said, ‘Father! Don't you want to listen to all the things I went through?

I know you love me. Please, I need your help. Listen to me.' I tried to tell you about all the things which happened to me through the years and all the difficulties I encountered.

"Then, slowly, as I was talking, I had the feeling that you were listening, although your eyes were closed. At one point, you opened your eyes and you looked at me. I was pleading with you, 'Father! Please, I need your help!'

"You looked at me and said, 'My dear child, I can't help you now. You have to help yourself.'

"Those words were ringing in my ears. And they are still ringing in my ears after so many years. I understood then, and I understand now that I have to help myself because nobody else can solve my problems. It was a message which you gave me. But now you are here. Please help me!

"You looked at me and to my great surprise you said the same thing, 'I came to tell you that you have to help yourself, that you have to have faith in God. You are never alone. You know that Almighty is watching over you at all times. I am now in Heaven and I always listen to you and ask God to care for you. Remember that you never have to be afraid. Didn't God help you in the German concentration camps? You survived. He gave you a second chance. He watched over you through all the years. He gave you the talent to write music and poetry. My message is: Develop your talents fully and have faith and courage. Life is beautiful. Know that my spirit is always with you. You are my child, my love. I watch over you beyond the grave. And now, I must go.'

"Again, I pleaded, 'Father! Please don't leave me! I don't know what to do.'"

My father said, "My child, I have to leave you now. And you go back from where you came. Here is the angel who is going to lead you to the right path. Follow her." With that, my father disappeared.

Immediately, the angel was at my side. She stepped up to the podium where I was and said to me, "Give me your hand. I will lead you. Just follow me."

I took the hand of the angel. Together we walked out of the synagogue. And then I wanted to hold onto the angel. But she said to me, "I will go in front and you follow me."

"Angel, I feel so weak, I want to hold onto you."

"You have to be able to hold onto yourself. Just run and follow this path in front of you." With that the angel disappeared.

I was again there in front of the synagogue and I could see the same path which I trotted before. I shouted, "I don't want to go back to the same path! I don't want to go back to the same place because I will never find my true self. How can I find my true self?"

Suddenly, I heard a voice within me, *I am your true self. I am here.*

"True self, what should I do? Please guide me."

Run, now … Just follow the path.

"My true self, I am scared. How am I going to find my way?"

You will. God is watching over you. Listen to your true self. Remember, you always had faith in God even when you were a young child. You were never afraid. You always did the things you wanted to do and you knew by then that God was always with you. Return to that knowing. Your true self is always with you when you believe in God's assistance. Your true self is the one who has faith in God. Your true self is strong. If you want to find your true self, then you must believe in yourself. You have to follow your own direction.

Then, my true self was silent, and I knew that I was on my own.

Once again I ran desperately. I told myself, *This time, I am not going to veer off to the right or to the left. I will just run straight ahead.*

The fall landscape repeated itself. I could see again the fallen leaves and rusty grass on desert ground. Then in the distance tall trees appeared. I kept on running for what seemed a long distance. I got so tired. It was already evening and I saw the lights of a city. I surmised that it was the city I had started from.

Although it seemed that it was getting later and later at night during my run; as I approached the city, more light appeared, actually, a very bright light. As I came closer, I could see the sunrise. When I arrived at the city, I was sure that it was the place from where I had started my run, and I felt utterly confused. I could distinguish the people and the familiar streets coming into view.

Then, as I entered the city further, its streets suddenly disappeared. It was like a repetition of my previous experience. A dense fog surrounded me again and I couldn't see anything. I told myself, *The same thing is repeating itself over and over. It seems that after all that has happened to me, I got nowhere.* I was desperate and cried out, "My true self! Where am I? What's happening to me again?"

But my true self was silent. Strangely, I could hear the voice of the angel. "Don't be afraid. God is with you."

"Oh, Angel, Where are you? I know you are a sacred spirit sent from the sky. Tell me what's happening. I am in the deep fog and I can't see anything. What is that?"

The angel said, "These are all the tears that you've shed. Look. Can you see anything in this fog that you didn't see before?"

"Angel, I can't see anything."

"God will clear the fog. You've shed enough tears. Stop your tears and look around, and you will notice that the fog will gradually dissipate." I heard the angel's voice, "Now look. What do you see?"

Before me stood my family—my husband, my children, and my mother! I said, "My God! It is my family!"

I could hear the angel's voice, "You find your true self in your family. Your true self is not only you, it is also your family."

"My mother is here and I know that she died four years ago!" I exclaimed.

Again I heard the voice of the angel. "Yes, but her spirit is always with you. She is residing in Heaven. She just wants to remind you that her love never died. She is always with you, just like your father, who is now in Heaven, too. Your mother wanted to see you and talk to you."

I could hear my mother's voice. "My child, live in peace with yourself. Find joy in your family. This is your family which makes you happy. You are part of me and they are a part of you. I go back to Heaven, but always remember your true self. I know best what your true self is, because I gave you birth. If you want to find your true self, then feel the love and affection coming from your family. Keep your memories of me, of your father, and of your family members who are residing in Heaven. As long as you keep love and faith in your heart, you will always be your true self. Your true self never left you and can never leave you."

My mother disappeared, and I embraced my family. I asked myself, *What do I really want from life? Why did I go so far looking for my true self? Am I such an egotist that I only think of myself? I looked for my true self and never found her because she was with me all along. Maybe I had to go through all this in order to understand that my true self is not only me, but also my family.*

So we embraced each other and I felt such happiness, peace, and harmony descend upon me. Then, I heard a voice, "It's eight o'clock in the morning. Wake up, my darling." I wondered where this voice was coming from. So I opened my eyes and I found myself lying next to my husband in bed. He said, "You must have had a nice dream and a deep sleep. I tried to wake you earlier, but you were sound asleep."

I smiled at him and said as I embraced him, "I love, you, I love you, I love you!—You are a part of my true self!"

Visions

It is midnight,
Darkness covers my sight.
There is stillness, but I am restless,
Listening to the rhythmic ticking
Of my clock on the night table ...
I am unable to sleep.

Gradually I drop into the nest
Of complete emptiness,
And regress into nothingness.
No lofty thoughts enter my mind anymore,
I wonder what destiny has for me in store ...

"Where are you, Muse?
Divine Spirit of Inspiration,
Liberate me from this mental vegetation
And revive my desire and motivation
For the art of creation.
I lost my passion for creativity,
I stopped writing music and poetry.
What is happening to me?
My mind is obscured by fear and anxiety.
The past, the present, and the future
Have meaning for me no more ...
Depression is possessing my core."

I hear someone knocking on my door,
But I can't get my feet to the floor.
Shivers are running down my spine …
I can still talk,
Although I can't stand up or walk.
My voice is still loud and clear,
I can feel and hear …
Am I in a trance?
Did I lose my sanity?
What is happening to me?

In my fright and desperation,
I address loudly
The intruder who disrupts
My peace and privacy:

"Who are you stranger?
What is your intention?
Have you no decency or shame?
What is your name?
Are you the messenger of destiny,
Like the one in Beethoven's 5th Symphony?
Or just a friend concerned
And worried about me?"

Don't have any fear,
I am your guardian angel.
You can't see me …
Many times I come here
Watching silently

Over your safety,
Protecting your health and sanity.
I will pull you out from your dark hole
And save your body and soul
From deterioration.
My mission is the restoration
Of your literary creation.
Have faith in me,
I am at your side . . .
My will you have to abide.
Control your anxiety,
And have trust in me . . .
My intentions are honest and pure,
You will benefit from them for sure.

I am your friend . . .
Give me your hand,
And close your eyes.
You will soon find yourself
In spirit's paradise.
You will enter the deep recesses of your soul,
The spirit of self–knowledge
Upon you will call.

"My guardian angel,
Can you reveal yourself to me?
I want to see your gracious face
And your white wings of purity."

Dreamworld

You can see me
Only in your dreams,
Along serenity's peaceful streams.

Listening to the soft voice
Of the saintly, ethereal manifestation,
I enter the world of imagination.
It seems like a hallucination,
Finding myself in a strange place
Which doesn't exist
On this earth's face.

I am standing in front of a golden gate …
A sign is posted upon the precious shiny rails:

In this ethereal place, silence and peace prevails!
This golden gate leads you
To your house of fate …
Pass through its massive door
And you will enter
Your life's corridor.

Two angels appear in front of me.
They take my hands
And accompany me
To the house of my destiny.

The heavy, massive, wooden doors
Of a strange, large building
Yield to the command
Of my saintly friends,

And open up widely.
As soon as I enter through them,
They close up promptly.
The angels disappear
And I feel lonely,
Filled with apprehension and fear.
I find myself enclosed
In a small, empty, dark room
Illuminated only by the shining, white moon,
Which peeks in
Through broad, panoramic windows.
Its bright face is staring at me …
I feel cold shivers running through my body.

A young girl dressed informally
In a simple, white blouse
And a black, pleated skirt
Appears in front of me.
I can't see her face clearly,
But I notice that she has long, chestnut-brown hair
Extending down to her knees.
Her eyes are sparkling and lively,
Although she is standing motionlessly
Like a statue on display
In some stately museum.
I stand in amazement, facing her,
Not daring to utter a single word.
A great uneasiness in my heart is stirred …
I wish I could fly from this place
Like a bird!

Dreamworld

It seems that even in the poor light
I can recognize this person from the start ...
She looks like me a long time ago.
This apparition of myself
Is addressing me kindly:

I am the spirit of your youth,
You are in the chamber of truth.
My duty is to bring you to your senses,
And to show you the world
Through my special lenses.
You left me a long time ago.
Since then you survived
The Holocaust, the fires of the war,
And all the difficulties
Which for you were in store.
Resent no more
The injustices and suffering
Which were inflicted upon you before.
I came to remind you
That your life has to go on,
So try to have joy and fun!
Leave your old, unpleasant memories behind,
Let them stay dormant
In the depth of your mind.
Listen to me,
And let the force of life
Supply you with fresh, new energy.
Be wise and clever,

Don't hang onto me forever.

Don't evoke me constantly.
Please grant me peace,
And release me from your grip.
Let me fade away
Into the hidden past.
Your life will not forever last,
So remember to live in the present!
And now, step forward
To the next compartment.
After I lead you there,
Let me vanish into thin air.

Before I could answer
My former identity,
She opened another door for me
And then disappeared suddenly.

I find myself lying
On a concrete floor
Surrounded by a raging fire.
I ask myself in terror,
Will my life soon expire?
Was I brought here to perish?
I can't control my fear,
Nor my anguish.
I am terrified and I cry out loudly:
"What is the reason
For my captivity

In this hellish prison?
I am innocent!
At no time
Did I commit any crime!
Is there anyone here
To liberate me?"
I hear a voice speaking to me clearly:

This is the prison of your house of destiny.
You are here to learn to cherish
Your freedom,
And to be instructed
In the principles of wisdom.

"But I will burn,
And thus never learn
The art of living!
I will be locked forever in Death's pavilion,
And fall into total oblivion!"

The flames promptly subside,
And an unearthly creature
Appears looking frightening and weird.
He has a long, white beard,
And four eyes upon his forehead.

He addresses me …
His voice is powerful, yet kind,
Not malignant or indignant,

Do you know who I am?

"I have no idea
Who you could be …
Can your many eyes
Foretell the future for me?"

I am wisdom
My eyes see the multi-dimensional
Aspects of life.
They detect the hot flames
Of burning desires,
Raging like Hell's fires.
I see man's destiny,
And detect the fierce passions
Within thee.
I am here to keep you company,
Let's leave this place of doom and agony.
Come with me to the next room
Of your house of destiny.

I wonder what other adventures
Are awaiting me …
I am passing through
Another door,
And I enter a heavenly room
Where angels are singing.
I see the sun shining
Through the tall windows …

The saintly apparitions
Form a circle around me,
Singing the song of liberty:

Happy is the person
Who is free
From gloomy thoughts
And worry,
Who is content,
Whose heart excludes
The vile specters of hatred,
Revenge and jealousy,
Whose soul is filled with love
For humanity,
Who has the wisdom
Of living happily.
We sing for you
The Songs of Life,
Giving thus comfort
And good advice for thee.

At the end of the heavenly performance,
One of the angels comes to me,
Placing in my hand silently
A small, glowing torch.
Then suddenly,
All the angels disappear
And my thinking becomes unclear …

Why am I again
In an empty, dark room
Filled with foreboding and doom,
Illuminated only by my ethereal torchlight?
No one is in sight …
Is this place real?
Or is it an illusion?
I am in a state of total confusion!

For what reason
Are the flames of my torch
Extinguished abruptly?
It is becoming pitch dark …
What a somber sight!
I am enclosed in a stark
And dreary place,
Void of sounds and light.
I feel helpless and terrified,
Asking myself constantly:
Is destiny playing
Some nasty tricks on me?
Where am I?
Is there anyone listening
To my desperate cry?

"Where are you, my guardian angel?
Come and set me free
From this dismal prison
Of my house of destiny!
Let this room be filled

With your bright, ethereal light …
My protector, please come into sight!"

Gradually a blinding light
Encompasses my room,
Easing my fright and doom.
Heavenly music resounds
And fills the air …
I hear a voice coming from nowhere:

Don't panic, don't despair
I came to take you out
From your house of destiny
And set you free!

Elijah, my favorite prophet,
Clad in a white robe
Appears in front of me …
Is that heavenly apparition real?
Only an illusion?
Or my eyesight's distortion?
Elijah answers my question:

This is reality!
Come with me,
I will take you from here
To your true house of destiny,
To Heaven on earth!

Dreamworld

Open your eyes,
What do you see?

How can it be?
I am in my bedroom,
Lying on my bed
Next to my husband,
Resting my head on his chest,
Listening to his soft breathing …
In the next rooms
My son and daughter
Are still sleeping …

I am wide awake …
So, all that happened to me
Wasn't real after all …
It was only a fake,
A strange dream,
It would seem …

But then I can hear
Elijah whispering in my ear,

Know you are in the right place,
Accept it with gratitude and grace!
Be happy, appreciate and enjoy your family.
You are now in the true house
Of your destiny!

Although I can't see Elijah around,
I feel that he is with us,
Not only in Heaven,
But also here on the ground,
Bringing us happiness and protection.

My heart is filled
With so much love and affection ...
I press my lips softly
On my husband's cheek.
The morning's streak of light
Illuminates his face,
And I know that
I am now in the right place,
In the true house of my destiny
Assigned for me.

When he opens his eyes
And looks at me,
I am in Heaven's Paradise,
Free of frustration and worry.
My thoughts become clear,
No longer blurry,
The spirit of happiness
Resides within me.

Providence

Destiny was playing tricks on me on that particular beautiful Saturday morning. It was the driving force pushing me in a certain direction. Not knowing why, I decided to go with my inner urge to stray away on that day from the familiar streets of the city and explore its many side streets. I was sure that I would find my way back no matter what. In my wanderings, I came to a very narrow street and, as I followed it, I realized that I was on the outskirts of the city. It was very deserted. I couldn't see any people on the streets and the houses looked so silent as though everybody was asleep. I looked at my watch; it was ten o'clock. I wondered, *Is it possible that everybody gets up late?* But I continued on.

Then a strange thing happened. The houses disappeared and in their places tall maple trees emerged displaying their colorful, vibrant fall colors. I couldn't understand how that was possible, considering that when I left home just a short time before, it was a beautiful day in summer, the sun was shining, and the trees were clad in their luscious green foliage—it seemed that somehow in a miraculous and inexplicable way, I stepped into another season.

Nevertheless, I kept on going and the houses once again came into view, but I had the feeling that I was not in the right place. It looked as if I had entered another city—but I still continued walking. Again, the houses were deserted and there were no people on the streets. I could see tall maple and elm trees. A strong wind started blowing, stripping the colorful leaves, painted by autumn's wizard, from the old branches. As I went further the landscape had turned into late fall. It was also getting cooler because the wind had picked up. I looked at the skeleton-like, bare branches of the trees lined up along my way. I realized that I was totally lost in that desolate, fall landscape depicting the end of November. I didn't know where I was anymore or where I was heading.

My first thoughts were that maybe in the worst case, I would knock on one of the doors to ask somebody where I was and, perhaps, someone would give me directions to get back to the city where I was residing.

Then, as I walked on, I looked back. Upon doing so, I saw a long line of men and women, looking pale and haggard. And they looked like prisoners. Their backs were bent as if they were dragging something, but I couldn't see anything behind them. They were dressed in rags. In front of them stood a blond woman dressed in a uniform that was familiar to me.

As they came closer, I heard the moaning of the people. I thought that they must have suffered a great deal. The moaning grew louder and louder. Although I wondered who they were, I figured that at least it was good to see some people. Maybe I could get directions from them. The blond woman in front was smiling. She came to me and asked, "Where are you going?"

I answered, "Frankly, I don't know where I am or where I am going."

Then she said, "Why don't you come with us?"

It seemed to me that she was the leader and I heard the people behind her telling me, "No, don't follow us! Stay away from her! Listen to us!"

The woman said, "Don't pay attention to them, just come along with us."

"Who are those people?"

"You are going to find out later. Right now, why don't you just join us?"

"Where are you going?"

"If you join us you are going to find out." She took my hand and said, "Come, come along." Then she took hold of both of my hands and started pulling me.

As we walked, I heard the moans and the warnings from behind, "Don't listen to her. Don't come with us. Get away!"

There was something strange in all that was happening to me and I thought, *Perhaps, I should listen to those people. Maybe they are trying to warn me.* I tried to get away, but at that point the woman grabbed my arm and said, "You just come with us!" This time I felt that she was forcing me to go. Now, she was not only smiling but she was laughing, and I couldn't get away from her grip.

We went farther and farther. The houses disappeared. I heard the moans of the people, "You made a mistake. You didn't get away when you could. Now you are trapped."

I realized that those people were right; I was trapped to a certain degree.

She looked at me and smiled, "Don't listen to them."

Then I felt horrified, because the line of people reminded me of the German concentration camps where I had been a prisoner of the Nazis, due to the fact I was of Jewish faith. I remembered a scene from Auschwitz-Birkenau, an annihilation camp where I almost died. I recalled the line of people I saw through the enclosed fence where I was together with other women prisoners. I could see a line of people dressed in rags, men unshaven and bent. They were bent because they were dragging the corpses of the innocent victims of persecution to be buried in the mass graves. The men in the group looked weak and emaciated. They were starving like we all were. They were crying out, "Women, can you give us a rutabaga?" If we had a small piece of bread, we would throw it to them. Many times I broke my little six-and-a-half ounces of stale bread in half and threw it to them. I could see the men fighting for that piece of bread.

Then, as I looked at this laughing blond woman, to my great horror I recognized her. She was Irma Grese, the blond Angel of Death—the terrible, sadistic SS woman (*Schutzstaffel*, which translates roughly to "protective squardon"—everyone knows they were not protective!) who many times had beaten the prisoners to death in the German concentration camps of Auschwitz and Bergen-Belsen. She was the assistant of the infamous Nazi criminal, Dr. Josef Mengele, chief SS physician and selector of the Jewish people whom he considered not useful—infants, children, old people, sick people, invalids, pregnant women, etc.—to be sent to the gas chambers. He sent many of my family members, who fell into this category, to their deaths.

I had been selected for slave labor for the gruesome task of dragging the corpses of innocent victims, digging the death pits, and incinerating their bodies. The four crematories, although working full time, couldn't handle the daily quota of over 20,000 bodies. Mengele also had his infamous laboratories in Auschwitz, selecting prisoners to be used as guinea pigs in horrible, criminal, medical experiments. Where Josef Mengele and Irma Grese appeared, death followed and raked wildly.

At that point I wanted to get away with all my might, but I couldn't because she was dragging me with such force that I had to follow, and I realized that I had made a grave mistake. If I hadn't strayed away from the familiar streets I wouldn't have gotten into such a predicament. Fate had been the driving force, pushing me in that direction. As we went along, she continued to drag me. I repeatedly heard the laments of the people, "You made a mistake. Now you can't get away."

We walked for a long time and finally we arrived at a place where there was nothing but barren ground. But then, I saw a huge pot with giant, red-blooming flowers in it. They were so beautiful, so unusual, so exotic. It seemed to me that there was a platform on which the pot with flowers was standing. As we walked in front of the pot, suddenly all the beautiful flowers wilted. Then, suddenly, the platform on which the pot was standing sank. We were facing the entrance of an underground of some sort, next to the edge of a deep hole in the ground. Then I came to a frightening realization: we had entered a grave.

But I had no choice. Irma Grese was dragging me with such a force that I couldn't get away anymore. Suddenly the sunken platform above us was lifted up and shut tightly by invisible hands. We were lowered into that underground passage filled with pale, emaciated-looking people. They were lying on the ground and moaning, "Why did you come here? Why didn't you stay out? You were tricked just like us." I wished that I would have followed the familiar streets of my city. I realized that fate was merciless to me.

Then, as we passed by all the people, there was somebody whom I recognized among them. It was my grandfather who died many years ago. He had been a successful businessman, very much liked. I asked my grandfather, "How did you get here? You were such a successful businessman, couldn't you find a way not to get into such a predicament?"

He said, "I could not make any business deals with death. I had no protection, I couldn't work out anything. You made a mistake to come here; you were tricked. But I hope there is a way that you can get out. I would like to see you, at least, getting out of here."

But Irma Grese had a firm grip on me. She only hesitated long enough to let me talk to Grandfather and find out the truth about where I was and what my fate would be. At this point I still didn't know exactly what would happen. She dragged me deeper and deeper into an underground place and finally we came to a big furnace. It looked like one of the crematories in Auschwitz where Jewish people were gassed and cremated daily. In spite of the fact that I also was Jewish, I had survived. I had survived three death camps: Auschwitz-Birkenau, Bremen, and Bergen-Belsen.

I wondered why I was again subjected to such a frightening experience. I couldn't understand what was happening to me. Had destiny again placed me into the hands of the terrible Nazi criminals whom I had seen committing horrible crimes during my captivity in the concentration camps of Auschwitz-Birkenau and Bergen-Belsen?

She opened the door of the furnace and I could see a raging fire inside. I knew what she intended to do: she would put me in the crematory, too. But at that point I was possessed by a great force—a force greater than hers. I broke away from her arm, which was holding me tight. I started running and running at full speed, but the underground place was vast and it looked as if it had no end. Many times she almost grabbed me—she was that close to me.

I heard a voice coming from nowhere, "Follow the light! Follow the light!" I ran in a straight line, with Irma Grese running close behind. As I ran, I could see a small flicker of light which was becoming brighter and brighter. Finally I could see that it was leading to the exit of the underground. Irma Grese was almost catching me ... almost catching me. Finally I reached the entrance of that big underground. I understood now where the light came from in that dark grave. The platform that closed after us when we entered the passage was now open. I jumped out from it with lightning speed. Irma Grese wanted to grab me, but at that moment the platform was pushed down by an invisible force and she couldn't follow me anymore. She was closed in the underground with all the others.

Then suddenly the big pot with the beautiful flowers appeared on the wooden platform. The exotic flowers were blooming again. I couldn't understand what had happened or where I was.

There were people around, but nobody paid attention to me and I thought, *Am I alive? Why don't they pay attention to me? Maybe they don't see me.*

I heard a voice, "You are alive. They are going to see you. You were saved by God."

I looked up and I could see Elijah, my favorite prophet. He appeared so many times in my dreams and so many times I found consolation with his appearance. There he was again!

Elijah said, "Don't be afraid. You are alive. You were saved. Look, tell me what you see."

I replied, "I see these beautiful flowers and I don't know what they are. I never have seen anything like them in my life. What are they called?"

He answered, "These are the flowers of life which are blooming again for you." With that, Elijah disappeared and I started walking.

As I walked, I tried to get back to the place where I lived. Gradually I could recognize again the familiar streets of our city and the people who were so happy to see me. They asked, "Where were you so long? We thought that something bad had happened to you. We feared that you were dead. We are so happy to see you coming back."

I said, "Yes, I was saved. I came back from the Labyrinth of Death."

I walked happily on the familiar streets of my city. Again it was a beautiful summer morning and I could see the flowers blooming. I felt such a joy and happiness in my heart. I said a prayer to Almighty, thanking Him for keeping me alive.

The Best Friend of Life

Why is your smile
Constantly aborted?
Why are your thoughts
So somber, diffused and distorted?
Why are you hiding
Behind your self-imposed prison?
Why don't you listen
To the voice of reason?
Get away from
Your room filled with doom.
Go outside and inhale the sweet fragrance
Of the colorful flowers in bloom.
Feel the warm, bright rays of the sun
And all your unhappiness will be gone.

"Who are you, invisible intruder?
You have no right to tell me what to do!"

I am Hope,
The best friend of life.
I came to lend you my help
And to ease your strife.
Why are you so disturbed and in distress?
Why are you so sad and restless,

Not finding peace in your heart?
Did joy depart from your soul
And leave in its place
A black, gaping hole?

"I am confused, robbed of happiness,
My thoughts are futile and senseless.
I hear ceaseless, disturbing sounds
And off-key melodies
Resounding in my left ear.
They torture my senses,
Abolish my peace,
And block my concentration.
Hope, dear friend of life,
Can you bring me relief and salvation?"

I can, but you have to leave
Your confined place
And master your constant preoccupation
With negative rumination.
I will teach you the first lesson
In coping with anxiety, fear and obsession.

Come with me in your imagination
To the distant station
Of the high mountains,
And listen to the sounds
Of nature's magnificent fountains.

They will chase away
The unwanted, out-of-tune, haunting melodies,
And will replace them
With the pleasant, soothing sounds
Of the fresh mountain streams
With their enticing symphonies.

We will walk together
On the steep trails of the mountain slopes,
And watch the big horn sheep run and leap,
And the graceful mountain goats
Climbing the shoulders of rough boulders.
We will listen to the whisper of the wind
And to the song of the birds in spring.
We will look at the elk herds passing by
And we will hear the high-pitched cry of the picas,
The high-altitude dwellers.
Get immersed in the beauty of the Universe
And you will hear the songs of life
Echo in your ears.
The ethereal music will stop your tears
And annihilate your frustration and fears.

"Hope, tell me,
Are you still here?
Or did you already disappear?"

I am at your side
To be your protector, advisor and guide,
To comfort you,
To carry you through
Your difficulties, doubts
And insecurities,
Bringing you into the world
Of positive realities.

Have faith in me—
I will always keep you company,
Not letting you out of my sight,
Trying to make your future bright.
Be wise and follow my light—
It will illuminate your vision
And clear your frustration and confusion.

Strange Encounter

Although I was never interested in football, one day I found myself at a football stadium. I didn't understand why I had gone there, considering that I had not purchased a ticket for the game. Yet, I had a feeling that for some strange reason I had to attend that particular game. I noticed the amphitheater was completely empty when I arrived.

I also wondered why I had selected a seat in the middle of the last row when all the other seats were available. Nevertheless, my intuition told me that I had done the right thing. Something compelled me to sit there and simply wait. I was confident that sooner or later people would come and the players would also appear. However, I was concerned that somebody would ask for tickets. Trying to attend the game without paying for a ticket would appear dishonest. I didn't know why I was acting like that. Up to this point no one had arrived. I sat and waited for a long time but nothing happened.

I became confused and began to question whether I had come at a wrong time. Perhaps I had missed the date and there would be no game at all. Finally, I came to the conclusion that what I was doing was senseless and crazy.

Just when I was considering getting up and leaving, I sensed someone sitting next to me. As I turned my head to the right, there sat Robert Frost, one of the greatest American poets! Being a poet myself, I had great admiration for Robert Frost. His poetry had been a valuable source of inspiration ever since I had begun writing my own verses. I turned to him and said, "I feel so honored to meet you. I have great respect and admiration for you. I am familiar with all your poetry. I especially like the beautiful lyric poems in your first book, *A Boy's Will.* I would like to ask you for some guidance and advice concerning my writings, but before that I want to ask a question: Will there be any football game taking place here today? It seems that no one has come so far. I was wondering earlier if I somehow missed the date of this game, but it seems to me that your presence indicates that a game was scheduled for today.

"Since I have never been interested in football, I don't understand why I came to this game. It is such a popular sport in the United States and yet I don't seem to relate well to it, maybe because of its violent nature. I imagine that you must like football; otherwise you wouldn't be here today. I also wonder why I haven't purchased a ticket. I feel uncomfortable about it."

"I don't have a ticket either."

"What's the reason that you don't have a ticket?"

"Because they know me, they will let me in here without paying for a ticket. They will be honored that I am attending this game."

"Why did you pick the last row?"

"Because if I were sitting right in front, then everybody would try to interview me. I prefer to have a little privacy."

"I'm so glad that I chose the last row of this big amphitheater. I had been wondering all along why I made this selection, but now I am so happy I did. It was meant to be; I believe I was destined to meet you. I am so honored. However, I am wondering ... Why hasn't anyone come yet?"

"We have to wait. They will be coming. The game is going to take place and this stadium will be filled in the course of time."

Gradually more and more people came, and pretty soon the stadium was packed. Every seat was occupied.

Finally the players arrived. There was something unusual about their attire. All of them were wearing masks on their faces. Only their eyes and the shapes of their noses were visible. One group was wearing black masks and black sport uniforms; the other group was clad in red sweat suits and bright red masks covered their faces.

I said to Robert Frost, "I never have seen anything like this. What could be the reason for the weird appearance of the players? What kind of game is this?"

He clarified it for me. "Well, this isn't an ordinary football game. This is the game of life and death."

"Oh my God! What do you mean?"

"I mean this is the game of life and death. You will have no difficulty figuring out who will be the winners."

"Death. Death is always the winner, the ultimate winner in the game of life," I replied somberly.

Then the game started. It was a fiercely violent fight. I had seen highlights of football games on television in the sports section of the CNN news, but I had never seen such a fierce fight as the one I was witnessing. Indeed it was like a fight between life and death. I wondered what was going to happen.

At some point the players in the red collapsed. They were stretched out motionlessly on the ground. They looked dead. It seemed that the specters of death were the winners.

Then suddenly, just like in a dream, the whole scene changed. All the players and all the people who were present in the stadium disappeared.

Once again, only Robert Frost and I remained in the stadium.

I addressed the famous poet, "Tell me, please, what's happening? Am I dreaming all this? Am I real and are you real?"

He said, "Yes, we are real."

"How come everyone disappeared?"

"Death carried away all the players. There will be other games of this sort. They go on all the time."

"I have had enough of these games. I never want to experience anything like that again. It will turn me off totally from ever watching another football game. Not that I was ever interested in them, but my interest is surely much less than it ever was before. Why are we sitting here when everyone else has already left? Maybe we should leave, too?"

"No, let's wait. Pretty soon we will once again see this place filled with people."

"Is it going to be another football game of this sort? I hope not because I really wouldn't like to witness anything like that again."

"No, it is not going to be a football game."

"What will it be?"

"This will be a lecture and recital."

"So that's why all these people are going to come? They want to listen to your recital and lecture?"

"No."

"Then who will lecture and recite poetry?"

"You."

"Me? I have never done public speaking. I have been writing poetry for a number of years, but I'm not ready for that. Besides, I need to learn more craftsmanship. How can I get up in front of all these people? I'm going to make myself ridiculous."

"No, no. You have no choice now."

"Why don't I have a choice?"

"Because I am here and I want you to speak. I'm going to be the one who will introduce you."

"Robert Frost, you are my idol. I'm sitting next to *you* and I am going to read *my* poetry? People are going to compare me with you. I have to be a great poet myself in order to be introduced by you. I can't do that."

I could see that the stadium was filled with people. There was a silence. Everybody was waiting for me. I saw Robert Frost stand up, descend from where we were, and go towards the front of the stadium. I could hear him introducing me, "Ladies and Gentlemen, there is among us a new poet who will read her poetry. I don't want to disappoint you, but I'm not going to be the one who is reading poetry today. I want to give a chance to this new poet, to inspire her. For years I have been her idol. For years she has read my poetry and now she is writing her own. I would like you to listen to her."

I could sense the crowd's expectation and Robert Frost was getting a big applause. Then he came up to me and guided me down the stairs to the front of the stadium. I found myself standing in front of the throng of people. I was terrified.

Then the whole scene changed. Again I found myself next to Robert Frost. I asked him, "What is happening?"

He said, "Just sit here now for awhile because there is somebody else who wants to say a few words about you."

I saw someone from the crowd getting up and going to the podium. It was a middle-aged man with dark hair, dark eyes, not tall in stature. He was wearing blue pants and a white shirt. He looked very informal, with no jacket. He said, "I would like to announce a new poet among us. As you heard before, Robert Frost thinks very highly of her. Please give her a big applause."

I heard the public applauding and I said to Robert Frost, "I can't do this."

He asked, "Why? You have to do it. You have to give it a try."

"Because I have never done public speaking! I am terrified!"

"You shouldn't be afraid. You should face the things which challenge you. You have no reason to be worried."

The crowd waited and waited, but I continued talking to Robert Frost because I was still anxious and in shock. I saw again this middle-aged man coming out and saying, "Well, there will be a ten-minute delay. Please be patient."

I thought, *Oh, God, please help me! I need these ten minutes to talk to Robert Frost about how I should do this.* Then I said to him, "I have to learn more about craftsmanship. It will be a long time before I can consider myself a true, accomplished poet. I might never be like you, but still I would like to be more accomplished. What about my craftsmanship?"

"Craftsmanship? The most important thing in writing is what you feel. The heart of poetry is more than just craftsmanship. I admit you have to be a better craftswoman; but the first thing in poetry, or in any writing, is sincerity, what you feel, and what you want to say. Go on! Have confidence in yourself, and that will give you the encouragement to share your thoughts and poetry with the people. Tell them what creative intelligence is. I know you can do it. Don't wait for perfection, because you are always going to feel that you have never mastered perfection. We always try for more and more perfection, but don't wait too long to share your poetry. Don't wait until you are too old for doing that. Now, get down there!"

Robert Frost, indeed, was very encouraging and I felt that I couldn't lose faith with him. So, although I was very frightened, I walked forward and found myself in front of the stadium, which was filled with people. They were waiting eagerly. I could not disappoint them.

I began my lecture and my poetry reading, "Poetry and Creative Intelligence." At that point, I gave way totally to my feelings, expressing what poetry is and what it means to me: "Poetry is my fulfillment in life. It is a great joy and happiness to develop one's innate creative powers, giving birth to verses and singing the songs of the Universe. It is like communicating with the unmanifested aspects of life and conveying them through the spoken words which rise from the immortal spirit. The creative process is to a great extent a subconscious manifestation. It starts with a vague and strange feeling. The birth of a poem is miraculous, mysterious, spontaneous, and natural. I can compare it best with the miracle of life. It is a sudden unexpected revelation.

"Creativity takes place in the silent chambers of the mind. Thoughts travel on the surface, but the Muse, the spirit of poetry, dwells in the depth. The soul is like a sea of life. The waves of thoughts constitute its surface and its silent depth nurtures the pearls of inspiration. In order to contact the Muse, it is necessary to dive below. My poem entitled 'Creativity' will serve as an illustration of this statement."

Creativity

In the silent sea of my soul
The waves of thoughts roll,
And upon their rising crests
My weary spirit rests.
While below
In the depths of solitude,
In their shells of isolation,
Float the pearls of inspiration.

"My perception sees the perfection and order in God's creation—everything and everyone has a destined role and a specific function. There is also harmony and coordination for smooth functioning.

"As I look at a rose I can feel its sap, its sustaining vital force governed by the Absolute, the same Absolute source of life which animates my body and soul.

"I can appreciate the different relative manifestations of the Absolute, like the delicate colorful petals, the green leaves, the stem, and the thorns. I understand that in the subtle strata of the rose is the root, which draws the nourishment for the entire flower. I can feel the whole entity of the rose sustained by the colorless sap which contains all the elements of the rose, just like a seed encompassing all the relative aspects of a tree: leaves, trunk, fruits, flowers, and roots.

"We are all flowers and trees in the garden of God, nourished by the sap of the Absolute.

"Writing poetry stems from a strong desire to experience the unmanifested sap of life, to expose the beauty of God's creation, and to appreciate all aspects of life.

"I want to feel a rose and communicate with it, to identify with it as a fellow creation of God. It has a different form and face than mine, yet it is carved and created by the same power. A rose looked upon in that context represents one of my life's partners.

"I can perceive the systematic order in creation also. A rose has its beautiful petals to be admired, its sweet fragrance to bring joy to the senses, yet it is also equipped with sharp thorns to be respected and protected.

"Through contacting and experiencing pure consciousness, I discovered the wide-angled aspects of a rose and I accept it in its full value.

"My poem 'Compensation' illustrates the duality, harmonious compensation, and unity of the whole of Creation."

Compensation

Is there anyone
Who scorns the rose
Because of its thorns?
Or, would you say
That it is less of a flower
Than a tulip born in May?
The sweet, delicate
Fragrance of a rose
Softens the sharpness of its stem,
Making it love's symbolic diadem.

After I finished my lecture and poetry reading, I could hear the applause of the people. Then suddenly everyone disappeared, and I found myself alone in the middle of the stage. I wondered if the whole thing had actually happened. Did I really give a lecture or was it a trick of my imagination? I looked up and I could see only Robert Frost sitting in the last row. I was looking forward to conversing with him again, but when I reached the last row he, too, suddenly disappeared. I found a small note on his seat. It read, "Soon we will meet again."

Then a mysterious thing happened. The whole scene disappeared, just like in a dream. I found myself in our bedroom, lying in bed next to my husband. I realized the whole thing was a dream. It was early in the morning and my husband was still asleep, but I couldn't sleep any more. I put on my robe and slippers and softly and silently opened our front door to retrieve the newspaper.

I went into the living room and sat down on my easy chair. On the front page of the newspaper there was a big photograph of Robert Frost, along with his biography and some of his thoughts on writing. I couldn't believe it. In that photo he looked just like I had seen him in my dream! I wondered what was happening. It was very strange. *Why did I have that dream? Why did Robert Frost appear in my dream? Maybe it was a message he wanted to convey.*

Then I remembered the football game. I could hear Robert Frost telling me, "This isn't an ordinary football game. It is a game of life and death which is repeated all the time and you can guess who will be the winners."

I could hear myself saying, "Death—death is always going to be the winner in the game of life."

It would have been nice if in my dream Robert Frost would have waited for me and I could have had the opportunity to talk to him after my presentation. I would have liked to hear his comments on my lecture and poetry recital.

As I was reading the article in the newspaper about him, somber thoughts crossed my mind. I thought, *We are merely visitors on Earth and our destiny is carved at birth. One day we have to go away to the other side and leave life behind. Death is the ultimate fate of man, the winner in the game of life. Each one of us has a certain life span which is preprogrammed at birth.* I hoped that my life span was going to be a long one so I could be a writer for many years to come, and maybe one day I could truly master craftsmanship.

I asked myself, *If my dream would have continued and if I were still in that football stadium next to Robert Frost, how would I express my thoughts on life and death to him in a poetic form? Would I be able to establish my own poetic value and style, forgetting perfect craftsmanship, and concentrating on my true feelings, on what I wanted to convey?*

As Robert Frost said in my dream, "The most important thing is writing the content of your thoughts, what you feel and what you want to say."

Robert Frost was and will always be a great source of inspiration for me. I feel that his message in my dream was to manifest my own poetic voice, to establish my own style, and to have the courage to convey it. I realized that I had to open my mind and heart fully to the mystery of creativity and to render my heart to my best guide—the Muse, the spirit of poetry.

I went into my study, picked up my pen and paper, and started to write the following poems about life and death.

Prologue

Life is but a brief encounter
With the joys of earthly fun.
On the wheel of fate
Our destiny is spun—
Delicate threads of ecstasy
Mixed with course fibers of doom and agony
Are woven on the loom of existence
By the invisible hands of Almighty God.
The finished cloth,
Stamped with our blood,

Never becomes our property.
We are allowed only
To take a short glimpse
Of its beauty,
Before death takes it away
At the end of our last day.

Farewell

Someday
We will have to turn
Away from life,
Stop our strife,
And leave behind
All the beauty
We did find,
And say goodbye
To all the earthly things,
To the sun,
And to the starry sky …
Dark night will prevail
At the end of our trail,
Where death will hail
Its victory …
Forgotten we will be.
But, the trees above
Will still go on
Providing shade, protection, consolation
To the other generation,

And the open prairie
Will still be the place
Where the restless souls roam,
Searching for fulfillments and goals,
While the grave will become
Our eternal, silent, somber home.

Triumph

Death celebrates
Its victory,
Marching wildly
Through the city,
Striking the young
And the old,
Beheading life
On its cold scaffold—
Then leaving behind
A severed mankind
Ridden with pain and agony,
The cruel specter retreats
To its kingdom
Of earth and stone,
Mounting its throne
Of human bone,
Waiting to launch
The next assault
On its constant enemy,
The live, pulsating body.

I put down my pen and went back to sleep, hoping that maybe I would meet the spirit of Robert Frost again in a dream so that I could share my poems with him. It didn't happen on that day, but I knew in my heart that we would meet again soon ... perhaps in my next dream.

Spiritual Conversation

Who is calling me
In the middle of this dark night?
Why can't I see anyone in sight?
Who is hiding within my dwelling place?
Intruder, declare your identity!
Reveal your face,
And clarify why you came to me.

I am Muse Euterpe,
The spirit of music and poetry.
My name is mentioned
In the books of ancient Greek mythology.
Through the years
Many musicians and poets
Were evoking me ...
I am your devoted, invisible friend.
I am here to lend you
My helping hand,
Bringing you joy, strengths,
Liberation from your worries
And frustration.
Come along with me
To the marvelous land
Of imagination.

My faithful companion,
Please, leave me alone,
Let me perish on sorrow's throne.
I am depressed, disillusioned and lonely.
Don't you see
My well of creativity is dry?
Therefore I want to die—
No more verses,
No musical compositions,
No fresh new ideas
Are for me in store.
I can't write, nor compose music anymore.

You can't chase me away,
With you I will stay.
I am here to appease
Your troubled soul
And to ease the torments
Of your mind,
So that you can find
Peace, happiness and harmony.
And thus you can return
To the Arts of Music and Poetry.
I am your spirit of inspiration.
Poet and composer,
Rise from gloom's station!

Poetry and music dwell in the core of your heart.

They can't be torn apart!
Emerge from the stormy sea
Of your soul
And fulfil your predestined role.
Have courage and confidence,
Patience and tolerance.
Conquer your anxiety
And return to the wonder–world
Of music and poetry.

My emotional pain
Is killing the dormant music and poems
In my brain.
Your efforts to comfort me
Are in vain!
It is senseless to continue my vocation.
Who will pay attention
To my artistic creation
After my life's cessation?
Who will care about the expressions
Of my spiritual identity?
Who will look into the mirrors
Of my true personality?

Don't you want to leave
Your image behind
For your family?
And your literary

And musical contributions
To society?
Think of the future generation
And stop your distress and frustration!

Tell me please,
How can I renew my desire
To light within myself
Creativity's fire?
I am not young anymore,
I don't know what the future
Holds for me in store.
What great miracles can happen to me?
Those are the secrets of my destiny.
I feel discouraged and tired
Of creating music and verses.
Who cares about my musical compositions
And my literary contributions?
Muse Euterpe, please help me
To find for my problems,
The right solutions.
Give me hope and wisdom
And assist me to return
To my spiritual kingdom.

Listen to me,
Your loyal guide,
And push aside
Your doubts and fears.

Have trust in the Creator above
And practice the art
Of Faith, Hope and Love.
Use your artistic ability
Bestowed upon you by Almighty
And reveal the beauty of the Universe
Through your music and verse.
Don't concentrate on recognition,
Neither on success or fame.
Don't be obsessed
With the perpetuation of your name.
Let the flame of creativity within you
Constantly burn—
That could be the greatest distinction
You will ever earn.

Maintain your confidence and pride,
Keep modesty and contentment at your side.
Don't stray away
From the right direction,
Assert your free will,
Don't ever stand still!
Be creative, hopeful and clever.
Ask the Creator
To be helpful and good to you—
He will make all your wishes come true.
Open your heart

To the Lord!
Pick up your paper and pen
And start to write—
I will not let you out of my sight—
I am your spirit of inspiration,
Your assistant and guide,
I will always be at your side.

Miraculous, mysterious,
Powerful and persuasive Muse,
Your wise advice I can't refuse.
Please stay with me
For a long time,
Restore my life's zest and prime.
Let the bright rays of creativity
Shine within me,
And together, let us combine
The content, the pulse and the rhythm
Of my newly born, living rhyme.
And let us create once more
A brand new musical score.

Night Visitor

It was a cold, dreary night
When the glowing-white moon
Was out of sight,
And the silvery stars
Were not shining bright ...
I was relaxing
In my easy chair,
Enjoying my living room's
Pleasant, heated air,
And watching the sparkling flames
In front of my face,
Rising from the burning logs
Of the fireplace ...
While outside
Strong, wild winds were howling,
Rattling my doors and window panes ...
The heavy rain was pouring its large drops
Upon the pavement and rooftops ...

My body was resting peacefully,
But my thoughts ran far away from me ...
They were roaming the distant fields
Of Past Memory ...
My spirit became engrossed deeply
In the flow of events
Of my past years,

Witnessing my joys and tears,
Following closely
My life's story
From childhood on,
Up to adolescence, adulthood,
Maturity, middle and old age …
When my thoughts finally reached
The stage of golden years,
A strange voice
Brought me back to reality …

Come with me,
I will take you away
From the territory
Of nostalgic melancholy
And self-pity …
I also want to spare you
From sinking into the deep, muddy ground
Of your past misery,
And from your excessive preoccupation
With all the happenings which took place
During your earlier life's station …

Who are you, invisible specter?
Why do you haunt
A lonely writer like me?
I don't want to have any dealings with you …
I can't learn anything new
By listening to your comments …

I take great pleasure in dwelling
On old events ...

I am your subconscious mind
Living behind all your thoughts and actions,
Steering you at my will
Into many different directions ...
I am also the Muse,
Your creative spirit of inspiration ...
I am a friend of your soul,
I am here to remind you
Of your assigned task and goal ...
Leave your present meditation
And follow me to the center
Of your inner being station ...

Writer, leave your imposed isolation,
Don't just be a dreamer ...
Your life will not last forever!
Therefore, take time to live in the present
While you are alive,
And develop fully
Your Heaven-sent talent ...
You are destined to be
The representative of music and verse ...
Let your spirit submerse
In the beauty of the Universe,

And in the wonderful world of fancy . . .
But also keep in mind and don't leave behind
The people and the real world around you.
Give up your constant
Self-examination, depression
And misery . . .
Go to your desk,
Pick up your pen,
And try to write
The best you can . . .

My good and loyal friend,
Thank you for lending me a helping hand!
Let's walk together
Through the ports of a bright future
And start a new adventure …
For awhile I am willing to leave behind
My obsession with the past,
And I will try to ignore
What destiny will cast
Upon my body and soul …
I hope that my old age
Will last for long,
That I will be for many years
Able and strong in mind and body,
And that my life will be filled
With happiness and creativity …

Writer, go forward,
Don't look back!
Then you will be
On the right track!
Let us work now together,
That will make your life
Happier and better . . .
I will never let you down.

I must leave at the crack of dawn . . .
But I will return to you each night
To keep you company,
And to supervise
Your music and poetry!

Tricks of Destiny

Ever since I was a child, I've had a great love for all the trees. My grandparents lived on the outskirts of the city of Cluj, located in the northern part of Romania. I was born and raised in that city which was and still is the capital of Transylvania. I resided there with my parents.

I left my native city a long time ago. I'm a survivor of the Holocaust. Being of Jewish descent, I was taken to the German concentration camps with my family when Hitler occupied the northern part of Transylvania, including Cluj, in March 1944. I survived Auschwitz, Bremen, and Bergen-Belsen, an annihilation camp, where I almost died. When I was dying in Bergen-Belsen, in the birch forest where the camp was hidden, those birch trees were my only consolation during my terrible captivity.

In the camps we were killed by starvation, and we had to drag the corpses and dig the death pits to bury all our dead. People were dying every day of starvation and infectious illnesses. On the day when I couldn't drag any more corpses and I was lying desperately on the barren ground of Bergen-Belsen, I thought I could die peacefully if I could hold and embrace a living thing for the last time before I fell into oblivion.

It was April 15—next to me was an old birch tree. I looked up at it and I could see the buds on its limbs. It was the only living thing near me. I wanted to die, embracing the wrinkled trunk of that old birch tree.

But God had other plans for me and I was liberated. After I was liberated, I remained there for half a year recuperating. It took me three months to recover from the effects of starvation. Then I spent time walking in the forest and those old birch trees became my friends. I lived in a world of memories. I was afraid to even think about who might have survived in my family, because I feared I wouldn't find anyone alive.

I wondered, *Why were we persecuted? Because we were of the Jewish faith? Why did that happen to us? Why did it happen to me?* But I had to accept it as the will of God, as my fate. I walked every day, amidst the birch trees, reciting the poems of my favorite great Hungarian and Romanian poets, like Ady Endre and Georgiu Coşbuc. I had studied in both Hungarian and Romanian schools, because the northern part of Transylvania where I grew up changed hands several times. I knew those beautiful poems by heart. Those were the moments when I felt such happiness.

While I was walking in that forest, I remembered my grandparents' orchard. My grandparents had lived on the outskirts of the city of Cluj in a big house. Because they had twelve children, I had lots of cousins to play with. Many of them died in the German concentration camps. During those walks, I remembered the old pear tree in my grandparents' yard. Oh, I loved that tree! It was an old fruit tree with beautiful Bartlett pears, and those pears were so juicy and so good. When we were little kids we went into my grandparents' yard with my cousins, and we collected those pears. When they were ripe, all you had to do was shake the tree a little bit and the pears would fall down. We gathered them in our little baskets which were given to each of us.

I still remember the old pear tree, even at my age, and I'm a grandmother now—I'm not a young person anymore.

The Old Pear Tree

I still remember the old pear tree
standing majestically
in my grandparents' yard
when I, as a small child,
playing with my cousins in the room,
suddenly flew out of the house fast
like a witch on a broom.
We shook the old tree violently,
waiting for its fruits to fall, impatiently.
We picked up the big pears quickly,
examining each one separately,
admiring their giant size,
uttering shrieks of surprise.
The good old tree
delivered us yearly
its produce faithfully.
We looked up at it with pride,
saying loudly,
"Here is the best friend
of Grandmother's yard!"
After all these years
our laughter mixed with tears,
still echoes in my ears.

Even now, after all these years, I still like to walk in the forest. I like the outdoors. Sometimes I feel that I can communicate with the different forms of life. Often, I will embrace the trees and I will caress their leaves. It is like holding hands with good, old friends.

After I came back from the camps and found my mother, I still liked to walk in the parks and in the forests of our beautiful city of Cluj. I found consolation with my old friends, the trees.

What made me leave my house on a cloudy afternoon in fall, when the leaves were changing? They were so beautiful. All of the trees displayed their kaleidoscopic foliage. The maple trees glowed with their scarlet-colored leaves. They were magnificent. I walked in the park. Why do I remember that walk in the park of so long ago? I remember my thoughts: *these trees are lasting longer than us.* I enjoyed these trees before I went to the German concentration camps and I enjoyed them again after I returned home at age nineteen. I ran among them, feeling happiness and consolation.

My life went on. After I found my mother, I met my husband Eugene in the summer of 1946. He was a medical student in his last year of study at the time. We got married that same fall. Then, at the same time, I entered medical school on a full scholarship. I was so happy because I always wanted to study medicine. I marveled at the human body and its mysteries. My father had advised me, "If you are Jewish, you better select a profession that is needed." But I didn't select this profession only because it was needed. I selected it because I had a love for it and I wanted to acquire all the knowledge I could.

After we returned from the camps—it was the Russians who liberated our city—we felt a gradual loss of liberty. It was the beginning of the time when our city was becoming a totalitarian place in which you were not allowed to express yourself. You had to keep your mouth shut, because otherwise you would be considered an enemy of the State.

At the end of 1947, two years after my return from the camps, we decided to leave Romania for Palestine, which was under British mandate at that time. It was an illegal emigration from the British point of view. Our ships were confronted by five British battleships on the Aegean Sea. We were taken to the island of Cyprus, where we were imprisoned behind barbed wire for the next twelve months.

In January 1949, we finally entered Israel and soon after our son Henry was born. Five years later, our daughter Monica was born. There were hard times in Israel; the whole country was in a great economic depression after the war and there were housing shortages. My husband worked as a neurosurgeon there.

In 1957, we decided to emigrate to the United States. We wanted to create a better future for our son and daughter. Our son, at the time, was eight years old, and our daughter was three.

Now, as I write this, it is 1997. So, for quite a few years, we have been in the United States. Both our son and daughter grew up here. My husband practiced neurosurgery as he had in Isreal. We lived for awhile in the South, in Augusta, Georgia. Then we moved to Wisconsin, where we lived for sixteen years. And then we moved to Dubuque, Iowa, where we stayed for eighteen years. My husband finally retired, and we are living now in Fountain Hills, Arizona.

As I write, we are staying in Colorado, in the summer of 1997, eight-thousand feet high in the mountains. I love the mountains—they are magnificent and grandiose. They give you a true assessment of yourself. They point out that you are just a tiny little creature, created by God in a vast Universe.

I still love the trees. Now I'm among pine, spruce, and aspens. Those aspens remind me of the birch trees of Bergen-Belsen. I love to hike in the forest with my husband and admire all the beauty which surrounds us.

I became a writer through the years, because I wanted to be able to communicate with the outside world and with my inside world, with my soul. I felt that I needed to get to know myself. I get inspired from the outside world, from the things I see; and from the inside world, the invisible world, where I can't see what's going on, but I can feel.

I was always a dreamer. When I was a little girl, we would visit my mother's aunt and uncle, who also died in the concentration camps. I was taught to always be a good girl. If I went somewhere with my parents, I knew that I was never to touch anything, but to just look. I remember the knick-knack cabinet with glass windows where my mother's aunt kept many knick-knacks—little dolls, little baskets, some statues. I had a great admiration for those knick-knacks. I knew that I could not touch anything, but I looked and I looked. I imagined that everything came alive and talked to me. That fondness for knick-knacks still remains with me.

I've always had a rich imagination and I hope that I will never lose it. What happened to me one day was very strange … and this happened to me in my old age. At this writing, I am seventy-one years old. Sometimes, I wonder: *How did all the years pass by so fast? Where am I now? Who am I? Do I really know myself well?* Sometimes, I think that there are so many things that I still have to explore. And I still have to explore the depths of my soul.

One day I wanted to go on a walk in the city where I'm living now. I left the outskirts of the city and I ended up in a birch forest. That was odd, because I am living in Arizona. *How could I walk into a birch forest here in Arizona?* I wondered. Nevertheless, I loved those birch trees and they reminded me of the birch trees in Bergen-Belsen.

The only tears that I shed when I left the camps on my repatriation day were for my friends, the birch trees. But now as I walked among them, they changed before my eyes into huge maple trees. I could see again the beautiful change in colors, the change of the leaves, and I knew it was fall.

As I walked deeper into the forest, there were other trees unfamiliar to me and I wanted to know their names. Wherever I am, I make it a goal to learn the names of trees. Even in Arizona, I learned the names of the trees. *Why can't I recognize any of these trees? They look so different.*

As I walked further, I found myself in a forest of giant trees, which were totally unfamiliar to me. Then, I stopped in astonishment. I had come to the largest tree I had ever seen and I wondered how old that tree must be. Then it seemed that gradually I entered into the fantasyland featured in my children's book, *Tales of the Magic Forest.* I wondered, *What is happening to me? Am I losing my mind? Am I dreaming?* But nevertheless, I was curious. I wanted to know what was going on. Besides, the trees were enticing me.

I came to a huge fruit tree. I could see large pears hanging from it. *Oh, I remember the old pear tree in my grandparents' yard! But the leaves of this tree do not look the same. Nevertheless, the fruits are hanging on and I remember from my childhood that just a little shake is all it takes and the fruits will fall.* I couldn't resist it. I shook the tree and a big pear fell off. I was just about to bite into it when I saw a little elf sitting by the trunk of the tree. He spoke to me.

"Do you like pears?"

I said, "I love pears."

"Well, bite into it. They're really good. They are going to give you a lot of energy. It's going to take you a long time to get out of this forest. Here, I have a little basket for you. Collect some more pears."

"Where am I? What is this place? Why does it have to take such a long time to get out of here?"

The elf said, "Can't you recognize it? This is the Magic Forest."

I said, "Is this really the Magic Forest?"

"Remember the book of fairy tales you wrote for children?"

"This isn't the same forest, because in the Magic Forest not all the trees are giant, except for the Wisdom Tree. And it is by far not as big as this one here."

He said, "You know why? Because through the years they grew and they changed."

"Why did they change?"

"Because things changed through the years. They aged, but they still remained beautiful."

"In my book of fairy tales, the biggest tree is the Wisdom Tree."

The elf said, "This is the Wisdom Tree."

"I am so happy that I came here, because even at my age, I don't think I possess enough wisdom. Had I been wiser, I probably wouldn't have made so many mistakes throughout the years."

"I'm surprised that you still want to learn wisdom at your age, but I can see your point. So, if you want to learn wisdom, I want to prevent you from making another mistake. The wise thing for you to do would be to leave this forest and to return to your home. I don't advise venturing further from here."

"I'd rather make my mistakes, but still learn more wisdom. I want to see what is beyond the Wisdom Tree, where this forest leads. Maybe on my way I will encounter some interesting creatures with whom I can communicate, just like in my book of fairy tales."

The elf said, "It doesn't seem to me that I can talk about wisdom to you. I cannot prevent you from exploring beyond this point. I stopped here in order to warn you not to go any further. I wish you would listen to me."

It seemed that I didn't have enough wisdom at my age of seventy-one. I still preferred to make mistakes and get new knowledge, rather than to stay ignorant. That was my philosophy. So, I followed the path beyond the Wisdom Tree.

To my surprise, as I was going further, the trees changed again. I never have seen trees like that in my life.

They became smaller and smaller, and as I proceeded on there were not even trees anymore, but bushes, flowering bushes. After awhile, the flowering bushes turned into smaller bushes with no flowers.

Then I came to what looked like a settlement. It had an ornamental gate and a fence. Such gates are especially popular in Arizona. Before you enter a house, there is a gate leading to a small little garden entrance decorated with some bushes and flowers.

I perceived a big area through the gate and fence. There were only small bushes and grass on the sides of this enclosed territory. There were also many benches. I couldn't believe my eyes—there were many bearded Santa Clauses sitting on those benches! I knew when I had left home, it wasn't Christmas—it was only October!

I was growing tired, but nevertheless, I was curious to learn why all these people were dressed up like Santa Claus. As they sat on the benches, it looked like they were conducting a meeting.

I said, "Hello, hello. I'm just a passerby here and I would like to talk to you. Actually, I am looking for some company. I feel pretty lonely. I've been walking for a long time and frankly, I don't know where I am. Would you mind if I asked for some directions?"

A Santa Claus came to the gate entrance. He was dressed in a red robe and a big belt from which tiny bells were hanging. He had a long, white beard and wore a red cap with a pom-pom on top. He made quite a noise, which reminded me of the Christmas song, "Jingle Bells." Strangely enough, when he started talking he sounded like a woman.

That is weird, I thought. *If that person wanted to be Santa Claus, she could have dressed up as Santa Claus's wife, wearing a feminine outfit. Well, maybe that's okay after all. Anybody can play Santa Claus.*

She opened the gate and asked, "Who are you?"

I said, "I'm a writer who was wandering in this forest. I was told that this was the Magic Forest. I was also warned not to come further by an elf who was sitting by a tree called the Wisdom Tree. But nevertheless, I was curious. I'm so glad that I followed my own instincts, because I got to meet you."

She was friendly and said, "Come in, come in. We're conducting a meeting. Before you join us, I have to ask permission for acceptance."

I could see her going to one of the Santa Clauses and talking for a short while. Then she came back and said, "It's okay. You can join us. Do you have any luggage with you?"

"Just one. And this basket of fruit."

"Oh, you have a small suitcase? What's inside?"

"Only some of my writings, all my favorite ones. I always carry these with me. I like to walk in the forest and sometimes I sit down and revise my work."

She guided me and said, "Here, sit down. You can join us and listen to what we are doing right now for a little while, before we settle you. You're welcome."

So I sat down. Next a very tall Santa Claus with a deep, baritone voice stood up and said, "Ladies and Gentlemen, you are well aware that we are conducting this meeting in order to set the rules for our settlement. Nobody can talk here unless asked. I am, as you know, the president of your group. We wanted to conduct a meeting to establish our rules but, considering that a stranger has entered our midst, we have to discuss whether we can give her shelter here and we need your votes on this matter. But before we do that, we will ask our strange visitor to declare who she is and why she came our way."

I stood up and said, "I am a writer and I always seek more knowledge. I left my home because I like the outdoors. While walking in this forest, by chance, I found your place. I'm very happy to be here because I was looking for company. Why do you all dress up like Santa Claus? It's not the Christmas season and I'm confused about that. Where am I and what's happening to me?"

Then the president asked, "What kind of things are you writing?"

"I am writing my autobiography. I am a Holocaust survivor and I am writing about my experiences. I also write fairy tales. I actually wrote a book of fairy tales called *Tales of the Magic Forest.*"

The president said, "We have to be very careful with writers, because they can instill doubt and they talk too much. They can do some damage to our settlement."

I said, "What kind of damage can I do? I don't write any political things or anything that would affect you."

He said, "You never know. Writers use symbols. Maybe it doesn't look like they are writing political things, but the characters in their stories may represent politicians or some aspects of politics or political criticism."

"I reside in the United States of America. Although I don't write anything like that, if I were to write some criticism, and I surely wrote some criticism about World War II and about my experiences being persecuted by the Nazis, it is allowed in our country. We have free speech."

He said, "That's exactly the problem. Your are no longer in the USA. Before you are admitted here, we have to revise your writings."

"I'm not willing to give out my writings. They are not even copyrighted. I don't want anybody to read them. Some things are very personal."

The president said, "In this place we don't allow things which are too personal."

I asked, "Where am I? Who are you?"

Then he asked, "Do you really want to know where you are and who we are?"

I said, "Yes. Who are you? Evidently, you are not Santa Claus."

Then I could see everyone around taking off their Santa Claus outfits. I observed that all of them were wearing uniforms. I thought: *What do these uniforms remind me of?*

I heard the president talking to me, "You should have listened to your little elf friend, because you made a big mistake. Do you know where you are?"

I asked, "What place?"

He answered, "You are in a totalitarian state where free speech is not allowed and surely you cannot stay with us unless we revise your writings. But you cannot leave this place either, because we suspect you to be a spy."

I said, "I told you before, I have never been involved in politics. I am not a spy!"

The president said, "It's up to us to determine that. Now, give me that suitcase!"

The woman who had let me in at the gate came and took my suitcase and even my fruit basket. She said, "You, come with me." There was no way I could run away, and I wondered, *Why did I come here? This is another place where people are robbed of their spiritual freedom and I can't accept living in a place like that. I don't want to stay here!*

But the woman grabbed my hand. She said, "I am very sorry, but you cannot get out of here before we revise your writings."

So I entered a room. It looked like a big office. A tall and muscular man was sitting at the table. He said, "Now let us see. … what do you have here? You have your book of fairy tales … we are very suspicious of fairy tales. Let's read a passage.

"First of all, on the first page, you say you are in a Magic Forest and you want to learn Wisdom. And then you have the Wisdom Tree, which reveals to you that you can learn Wisdom if you listen and communicate with all the creatures in the forest. This breaks our first principle: you cannot communicate here without permission. Before you communicate with other people, you have to communicate with me; and if I don't like your ideas, then you have to keep your mouth shut."

"I won't keep my mouth shut. I am used to the United States, where I can say what I think."

He said, "You came to the wrong place, because here you can't say what you think. Being a writer, you are the most dangerous person to us. You can be an enemy of our settlement here, bringing in new ideas, contaminating others with your freedom of speech. We can't allow you to do that. We'll have to burn your writings."

I said, "No, no, please don't do that! My writings are sacred to me. My writings are a part of me. It's just like killing a part of me."

"I'm afraid you have no choice. Before we give you shelter, we have to burn your writings. The first rule for you is to keep your mouth shut. You talk only when you are asked. And then, you say only what we want you to say, not what you personally think! You have to give up your identity here!"

I protested, "I don't want to give up my identity. I've been trying to keep my identity through all these years, even in the German concentration camps where I was tortured. Freedom of speech is sacred to me, and I don't want to stay here under these circumstances. I am sorry I ever came here. I should have listened to the elf. I wanted to learn more Wisdom, and instead I got into a place where ignorance reigns!"

The president warned, "You can't talk like that here. And, furthermore, I have very sad news for you. You can't get out of here either."

"I refuse to stay in a place where I cannot express myself, where my spiritual freedom is taken. I'd rather die and you are going to have it on your conscience. I'm going to kill myself if you don't let me out."

"Ah," the president said, "there is no problem in this. You don't have to do it yourself; we can do it for you."

At this point I was debating how to escape. I was in a prison where I had to do what they said, otherwise it would be the end of me. So I started lying. "I will try to understand you. Just please don't burn my books! Don't burn my writings. I will try to become one of you, although it is very hard for me."

He said matter-of-factly, "The only way you can stay here is if we burn your papers."

I thought to myself, *They can burn my papers, but I have a copy of them in my mind. They cannot take that away from me.*

He said, "We will give you a period of grace. You have to show a change; otherwise you will be tried as a traitor."

The woman, who had taken my suitcase filled with my writings, put me in a very simple room. She said, "There is another rule we have; no books, no paper, or writing instruments are allowed here."

I wondered what I was going to do. Then a thought hit me. *Maybe I can somehow befriend this woman. I will use my charm to start a conversation with her.*

I asked her, "How long have you been here?"

"For many years," she responded.

"Can you tell me anything about yourself?"

"No, I'm not allowed to talk about myself."

"Why?"

"Because by talking about myself, I will break the rules of our settlement and then I couldn't stay here anymore."

"Do you want to stay here for the rest of your life? You can tell me, because I'm not one of them. You can tell me how you feel about this."

"Here even the walls have ears. I can only whisper, because we cannot talk loud. I'll tell you frankly that I'm really fed up with all these rules."

"Well, you are not the only one! Did you ever think of escaping this place?"

"Many times it has crossed my mind, but I don't dare to do anything."

"If we collaborate with each other, we are going to have an opportunity to escape."

"How could we do that?"

"Somehow I have to get out through that gate and it seems to me that you are the gatekeeper. The gate is no doubt locked at night, but you have the key for it."

"Yes, it's true. I do have the key for it, but we are watched at all times."

"You are the only one who can help me. If you help me, we both can escape from here and go on our way."

"How are we going to do that?"

"There is one slight chance. Remember when I talked to you about the elf who was sitting by the Wisdom Tree, who warned me not to go further? My only hope is that the elf will help us."

"How can we talk to the elf here?"

"I've mentioned to you that I can communicate with nature. I can communicate with the trees. Although they are my silent friends, I can talk to them. So maybe I can somehow communicate with the elf on a spiritual, mental level. Did you ever hear of telepathy, or of spiritual communication? This is the science of the occult."

As I was speaking, I could see the door of my room was opening, even though it was locked. Somebody was opening it. I thought, *Oh, my God, somebody was listening to us; this is going to be the end of us.* But then the door opened and who came in but the little elf!

The woman who was supposed to guard me was very surprised. The elf said, "Talk to me."

I asked, "How did you get here?"

"I knew where you were, so I followed you, because I wanted to help you. Why did you want to learn the same knowledge that you have already mastered? I anticipated where you would end up and I came to rescue you."

"How are you going to do it? Please, if you're going to rescue me, help this lady also, who seems to be my friend. She said that she would like to get out of here herself."

"Sorry, I can help only you."

"Why?"

"You will find out later."

So the woman said, "No, you cannot rescue her. I am her guardian."

The elf replied, "You have no power over me!"

"What makes you think I don't have any power over you?"

"Because I'm a spirit that can't be harmed. You can't touch me."

She laughed. "You look like you are real."

"Try to hold my hand." Suddenly the elf became invisible.

The woman said, "Where are you? You little mischievous thing! Where are you?"

"I'm right here but you can't see me."

"Did you go outside? You are probably running outside where I can't see you."

She opened the door, trying to run after the elf. Although I couldn't see the elf, I felt a hand taking hold of mine. He was telling me, "Let's run. Come with me!"

I said, "She's going to look for me."

"No, she won't, she's busy looking for me."

And to my surprise, he opened the gate. I could see the woman running around frantically, alerting all the others and sounding the alarm. All the people dressed as Santa Claus came back again. But I was running away with the elf.

I asked him, "How come they don't run after me?"

"Because you are invisible."

"How could you make me invisible?"

"Remember, I have the spiritual power. Only your spirit exists now and your physical body is not visible. You are totally spiritual."

"I want to get back my physical body."

"Right now, you don't need it. Just come with me."

The gate opened and the Santa Clauses ran in all directions, but they couldn't see us. I was running with the elf and when we reached the huge Wisdom Tree, he said, "Wasn't I right? You should never have gone in that direction. You made a mistake."

"I realize I made a mistake, but why?"

"Because you are never satisfied. You look for new things, but you don't think before you do something."

"What should I do now?"

"You go home now!"

"But how can I go home now? I don't even know how to get there."

"Well, don't you remember the way you came? You came in a straight line. Follow the giant forest. Run. Run! Remember the Snowshoe Rabbit from *Tales of the Magic Forest*? She was a great runner, and she tried to take good care of herself. When she saw the fox she knew his intention was to catch her, and she realized the danger of being killed. She ran as fast as she could in order to protect herself—you have to do the same. You were a runner once, remember? See, I know everything about you."

"How do you know everything about me? You were living in this forest."

"Yes, but my spirit is free. Remember, I am spiritual. The only freedom you have is your spiritual freedom. So now, you are free to go. Get back to where you came from. By the way, where is your basket of fruits?"

I said, "Even that was taken away. They suspected me of putting poison in the pears."

"Before you go, I will give you a new supply of fruits. I will fill another basket with pears. These fruits possess wisdom. They contain the essence of wisdom in their juices, the wisdom that you need right now."

The little elf picked up the beautiful, giant pears, which reminded me so much of the pears of the old tree in my grandparent's yard, and placed them in my basket. I felt that now, indeed, I was back on the right path.

The elf said, "Sit down for a minute near me. Remember me, and eat this pear before you leave."

I trusted the elf. I knew that he was a good and kind spirit. I ate the pear he offered me and after I finished it, he said to me, "In the future, before you decide to take a trip on your own, before you head in the wrong direction, eat one of these pears and savor the fruit of wisdom."

I said, "But sooner or later all of these pears are going to be finished. What will I do then?"

"Yes. But then the essence of wisdom will be in your system and you will know right from wrong."

"How can I know right from wrong? I've done so many things I thought were right but they turned out to be wrong."

"Yes, but now you've tasted the fruit of wisdom. Go, now! Run back home!"

I started running and running through the giant forest. Then I heard the trees talking to me. "We are the Trees of Wisdom. By running in our forest, you will learn more and more wisdom, and by the time you get out of here you will have returned to your true wise self."

What's my true wise self? I asked myself, as I ran. I realized that I would be my true wise self if I followed my intuition and learned from my experiences. Then I probably would not repeat the same mistakes over and over.

As I ran, the trees became smaller and smaller. I came to the end of the forest, and I noticed a big well in front of me. I was very thirsty, but how could I drink water I couldn't reach? There was a pail on the top for people to use, but the well was so deep that I didn't dare to lower the pail. Suddenly, there he was, the little elf again!

He said, "I will draw water for you. Drink … go on, drink."

Then I came to a house. The house was so familiar, yet I knew I had never been there before; it wasn't my home.

Curiosity was driving me. I asked the elf for help. I said, "My savior, my protector, should I enter this house? It doesn't seem to be my house. Will I make a mistake again?"

He said, "No, you can enter this house with me. This is my house. It is the house of knowledge. Be my guest."

I followed the little elf into his modest home. The first thing I heard was beautiful music. I could see a piano in the middle of the room. The elf asked, "Do you hear this music?"

"Yes, I do."

"Listen—is it familiar to you?"

"This is Hayden's piano concerto. I played it once. What is this next piece? Oh, Chopin's mazurka. I also played that once. It is strange because I remember that I played it the same way as I'm hearing it now."

The elf said, "Yes, you played that a long time ago. I was there when you played it."

"How could you have been there? That was a long time ago! I was merely fourteen years old at that time."

He said, "Yes, but I recorded it and carried it with me."

I said, "How come I hear it now? Is that a self-playing piano performing it?"

"No, you are playing. Why don't you sit down and play now."

"I forgot how to play. I haven't practiced for many years."

"Go ahead, sit down and play."

"I don't know what to play."

"Play Chopin's mazurka. It will be easier for you."

I started playing. To my surprise, after all these years, I still remembered it. Then I heard the sound of a violin right behind me and I wondered who was playing the violin. I heard a voice telling me, "Don't play just the notes. Put some feeling into it."

I thought, *These are the words of my father. When I played that piece on our Spinet piano, way back when I was fourteen years old and he was accompanying me, he said to me, "Put some feeling into your music. Don't play just the notes."*

As I looked back, I could see my father playing the violin. At this point, I thought I was truly going insane. Not only did I hear my father playing the violin, but he talked to me. He said, "My child, I came to tell you to follow the spiritual path."

"Where is the spiritual path?" I asked him.

"The spiritual path will lead you to the study of music and poetry. Write your poetry. Write the verses to your music. Develop your true talents. I know best that it is the right direction for you to follow. Be a writer and a composer." And then he disappeared.

I asked the elf, "Where am I?"

"You are in the house of the spirits."

"How can I ever get home from here? Do I belong to this place?"

"You do. Give me your hand and I will take you home."

I took the elf's hand and then we were walking on streets which became familiar. I could see our home in Fountain Hills, Arizona. I came to our door. I saw the big cathedral ceiling in the hallway. As I walked into the house, I noticed that my husband and daughter looked very worried. They asked me, "Where were you for such a long time? We were worried about you."

"I was in the house of the spirits."

"What are you talking about?"

"There is such a house. I had the most wonderful adventure. I visited the Magic Forest."

They looked at me with genuine concern.

"You're acting strangely," my husband told me. "We think you're writing too much. You need a rest."

"Yes. … I walked right into my Magic Forest!"

"We are happy that you came home," my daughter said as she hugged me. "And what did you learn in that Magic Forest?"

"Wisdom," I replied with a smile.

Lonely Traveler

Lonely traveler, tell me,
Why are you roaming aimlessly
The deserted streets of this city
On this stormy night,
Exposing your body
To the harsh elements
Of this despicable
And miserable weather?

Wouldn't it be better
To stay in your comfortable home,
Instead of wandering outdoors and listening
To the roaring and frightening
Sounds of thunder,
And witnessing the blinding flashes
Of lightening?

What forces are driving you
To head to an unknown destination
In a state of confusion and desperation?
What strong disturbing emotion
Is pushing you towards
A certain unforeseen direction?

Dreamworld

Is this torrential rain
Somewhat cooling the heated,
Passionate thoughts
In your brain?

Can I help you today?
Find for you
The right way?
And ease the turbulence
Of your spirit?

My friendly stranger,
Please comprehend
That I am heading for No Man's Land,
Where the spirit is king.
There I intend to live
Till my days' end,
Looking for the true attributes
Of my inner being,
And for the Spirit of Freedom
And its House of Wisdom,
Leaving behind the world of conformity
And the rigid rules and regulations of society.

I want to be totally free to act at all times
According to my convictions,
Taking appropriate actions
Toward establishing my values
And having the possibility

To direct my own destiny—
Because after all,
I am a separate entity
And no one's property.

You are an idealist,
And not a realist.
Why do you fancy
That this imaginary world
You mention
Does exist?

I would like to draw
Your attention to the fact
That it is healthy, sensible and advisable
To live in the present and not in a castle of air,
Nor in the prison of despair.
It is very important
To use good judgment,
To accept the inevitable
Hardships we encounter
In our struggle for existence,
And to be aware of the need in our life
For endurance
And persistence.

By the way,
Are you running away
From your responsibilities?

Dreamworld

Getting lost in daydreams and fantasies?
To me it sounds unwise,
Unreasonable and foolish
To believe that we human beings
Can be spared and be exempt
From the leash of restrictions.

You should know
That wherever we go,
Our commitments,
Our obligations,
The rules and regulations
Of society,
And of our human destiny
Will follow us constantly.

Only death can liberate us
From our human bondage,
Offering us total freedom,
Eternal peace,
But robbing all our thoughts,
Feelings and knowledge.

I don't think
That you desire annihilation—
I doubt that your extinction
Will give you great satisfaction.

I certainly don't choose death.
Life is very precious to me.
I want to live and be creative
So I can dedicate myself fully
To spirituality.

But tell me, uninvited stranger,
Why do you follow me?
What are your intentions?
Are you also running away
From the world of conventions?

No, I am just lonely
And looking for somebody
To keep me company.
Man is not functioning properly
Without a friend or family.
Please let me keep you company
And watch out for your security.

So do you want to come along with me,
And leave behind the desolate world
Of loneliness and mankind,
And follow the way
Leading to spirituality?

No, I am a realist,
Not a surrealist.
I don't want to end up

On the ground of insanity—
I only tried to stop you
From becoming
A mental casualty.

Then leave me alone!
Go and shape your own fate.
Each person follows
His or her destiny—
There is a difference
In concepts and values
Between you and me.
In my world of fantasy
I am never lonely.
The imaginary figures
And apparitions
Keep me company.
I am not on the path
Of madness,
But on the road of fulfillment
And happiness.

Lonely stranger,
My persistent follower,
I want to introduce myself
Before we part.
I am a writer, a dreamer,
And a worshiper of art,
Yet also a realist, a fighter
And an achiever.

I carry within me
The seeds of duality and ambiguity.
I struggle for existence,
Asking for God's assistance.
I also pray each day
To Almighty
To send me from above
The precious gift
Of creativity and love.
Maybe someday
We will meet
On some unknown
Distant street.

Until then—
Look for somebody else
Who can provide
The company you need.

My rebellious friend,
I want you to realize
And understand
That we can't part.
I am the doctor of your soul—
To treat the ailments
Of your mind and heart
Is my goal.
You are in need
Of my services indeed!

Dreamworld

You need my advice and protection
On your way to your spiritual resurrection,
And my guidance to steer you
Into the right direction.

Therefore, my friend,
It is my decision
To lead you
To your wishful wonderland,
To that mysterious, strange domain,
Which can offer you
The joys of pleasure
But also the affliction of pain.

We shouldn't intend
To linger too long
In your fantasyland
Where things can easily
Get out of hand.
Long-term exposure
To excessive silence, total isolation,
Constant spiritual contemplation,
And lack of communication
With the human population
Can lead you to deterioration,
And to the loss of your identity
And sanity.

After our limited journey,
You will return with me
To the world of reality.
I want to save you from despondency.

I don't agree to the implementation
Of your plan and suggestion.
I don't accept the limitation
You intend to impose on my liberty.
You have no right to set my priorities,
Or steal my dreams and fantasies.
Who do you think you are
To tell me what to do?
I am sick and tired of you!
Please, leave me alone!
I can find my way.
I am the doctor of my soul—
I know best what is my goal.

I am sorry to say
That I am determined
To teach you
Courtesy and discipline.
I want to turn your spirit serene.
Believe me, I am your friend and guide—
I don't deserve contempt nor despite.
You hurt my feelings and pride—
I respect your feelings and aspirations,

I have full understanding
Of your desires, ambitions and frustrations.
Trust me, lonely traveler,
I know you better than you think.
There is a strong invisible link
Between you and me.
You don't realize that we are destined
To stay together—
We are like birds of a feather.

What is the purpose
Of our senseless discussions?
Are you trying to convince me
Of the dangers of excessive creativity,
Suggesting that I can lose my reason and sanity
By being reflective and solitary?
There is nothing wrong
In rejecting and running away
From the limitations forced upon me
By society,
Nor in the desire to live freely
In my world of imagination,
Away from the maddening crowd.
I don't perceive that
As my downfall,
But I consider it to be
My salvation
And regeneration.

I advise you to listen
To the Voice of Practical Reason,
And maybe in the course of time,
Hopefully before you pass your prime,
You will learn to comply
To some degree
To the restrictions imposed upon you
By the members of society.

Although you are a separate entity,
You still belong to humanity—
Therefore, you must face the reality
That you can't be totally free.
And you have to curtail your desire
To become a recluse
And an antisocial aberration,
If you want to survive
And make a living
On this earth's station.

Mysterious Stranger,
Please tell me
Who are you really?

I am a phantom
Of a special kind,
An imaginary figure
Existing only in your mind.

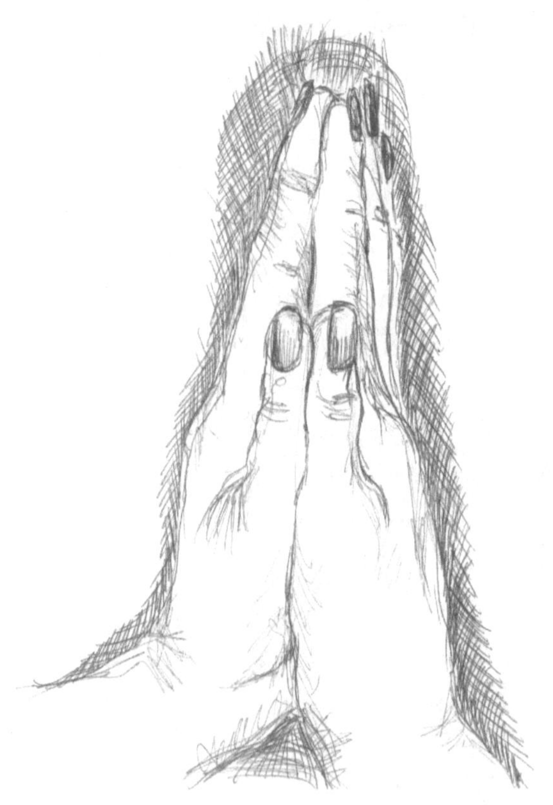

Thoughts on Life, Death, and Dreams

So often in our meditative states of mind we wonder what happens to us after we are gone. Life is so beautiful; it is never easy to depart from it. Everyone hopes to live a long time and all of us try to leave something behind us, because the thought that we are falling into oblivion at death terrifies us. So we try to do some things in life to be left behind and remembered, and each of us does that in a different way. Some people leave their artistic creations behind in paintings and drawings; some leave their thoughts in writings; others leave their beautiful handiwork. We hope in this way to be remembered. But will we indeed be remembered? Does not time efface and obliterate all our traces? As life moves on are we not forgotten? Nevertheless, we still have that urge to create something, hoping what we have left behind will keep our memory alive.

Great composers are not forgotten: Mozart, Beethoven, and others. Great writers and great poets like Schiller, Goethe, and Shakespeare are remembered through their artistic creations. By the fact that their works are performed, their spirits are alive and they are with us beyond their death. They remain alive through centuries, but not everyone is a Mozart or a genius. What happens to those who are not geniuses? We have to have a strong faith that somehow our spirits are going to survive, because otherwise we would lose all our motivation and desire to create something which we can call our own and through which we are revealing our individual identity.

Each religion stresses eternity. The Buddhists and the Hindus believe in reincarnation, claiming that our soul survives and then is reborn in another body. In the Christian religion there is the belief that there is a Heaven and we obtain eternity. We will deserve Heaven or Hell according to our actions in life. If we are righteous, we go to Heaven; if we are great sinners, we go to Hell. But has anyone come back from Heaven or Hell to tell us, if there is a Heaven or a Hell? Regardless, if you have a strong belief in God, you believe there is an afterworld.

I am of Jewish faith and in our religion we believe there is an afterworld. Actually, we believe that God judges us in the afterworld according to whatever we did in our life. So whatever good things we did in life, we are going to be rewarded for them, and the ports of Heaven are going to be opened for us. We must believe in the survival of the spirit. How could we otherwise accept the loss of our loved ones? We believe that although our loved ones are not with us, and their physical bodies do not survive (from dust we emerge, to dust we return), their spirits escape their bodies and rise above time and age, defying finality.

It was very painful for me to lose many of my family members in the German concentration camps. I was a captive there myself for one-and-a-half years because of my Jewish faith. My mother survived, but I lost my father and my beloved Uncle Eugene, who was a fencing champion of Romania. He did not have children of his own. He always treated me like his own daughter and, therefore, when I was five years old he wanted me to learn to fence. He was very strict with me. It was like having two fathers. I loved my uncle and so at age five, I started fencing lessons in order to please him. As a teenager I participated in fencing competitions.

At age eighteen I was taken to the German concentration camps with my family. When we were separated in Auschwitz my father said, "Remember to follow the path of love, forgiveness, and tolerance. Remember your father and take care of your mother. Cherish and respect her." My uncle said, "Remember, pain increases your endurance." So many times when I was fencing, I complained that my muscles were sore. He always said, "Pain increases your endurance." When I was doing horrible slave labor in the German concentration camps and lived in pain, that statement became the secret of my survival. I said to myself, *Pain increases my endurance and because of that I have to tolerate pain. I have to be a survivor.*

God rewarded me when I returned from the camps—I found my mother and had her with me for many years. She died in 1994 at the age of ninety-three. As I said earlier, I lost my father and my uncle in the German concentration camps in Dachau. My parents and my uncle were closer to me than anyone else in the world. They will always be part of me. I never overcame the loss of my father or my uncle. I had dreams about them both, dreams in which I talked to them.

The loss of my mother is still very fresh. The wounds are still painful. I still mourn all my family members who perished: my parents, all my uncles, aunts, and cousins. It was very hard for me to lose my mother because we were such good friends. She was ailing some years before she passed away and I took good care of her. Sometimes she said, "You are my daughter, but you are also like a mother to me." She deserved the best care I could give her. I would have given my heart to her.

When she died I went through great emotional suffering. Also, at that time, my husband retired—he had been a neurosurgeon for forty-five years. My daughter was recovering from surgery. Then I had an accident; I lost a part of the fingertip of my right middle finger, and I went through surgery. Then, we decided to move from Dubuque, Iowa, where we had lived for eighteen years. I had to face leaving my family and friends behind. I also had been a public speaker there for many years.

These were all difficult transitions for me. Just a few months after I lost my mother (who passed on March 27, 1994), I had a dream about her. Somehow I still feel that her spirit is alive. We never fully understand our dreams; we create fantasy worlds. But in my dreams is the only time I can see my deceased loved ones. So although they are no longer with me physically, I feel their spirits are always with me. I have very strange dreams where we communicate with each other, and they leave messages behind which I never forget. I remember them through the years, and I'm not a young person anymore! I have to believe in the eternity of the spirit because the older I get, I come closer and closer to my departure from this world.

My dear readers, I would like to share with you some of my dreams about life and death. Perhaps through this, you will understand that I do believe in the life of the spirit. Actually, I'm a very spiritual person because I am a writer, and what is writing? Writing stems from ideas, from thoughts. What are thoughts? Thoughts stem from our spiritual self, from the depths of our souls.

Let's begin with a dream I had shortly after my mother died. I dreamed that I was walking on a rough road filled with uneven stones. As I walked, it got worse and worse. It became muddy and the mud got deeper and deeper. I was heading somewhere, but I did not know where. In my dream, I wanted to go away somewhere, but I didn't know why. *What would be my destination?* I wondered as I walked. Besides a heavy knapsack, I was carrying two purses—I had no idea why I had two purses. The road became muddier and muddier. I stopped and thought, *I can't take this any longer. I just can't go any further. What should I do? I don't even feel like going back.* As I was debating what to do, suddenly my mother appeared next to me.

I was so happy to see her. In my dream I didn't realize that she was dead. She looked so strong and filled with vitality. I thought, *It is so strange that my mother at age ninety-three is filled with so much vigor.* She looked at me and said, "My child, you look so tired and you have such a heavy load with you. Two purses? What for? Give me your entire load. I will carry it for you."

I said, "Mother, do you want to carry my load at your age? Don't you see how heavy it is? And look at this road. I can hardly walk on it!"

She replied, "Just give them to me. We are going to manage."

To my surprise, my mother took my whole load and said, "Let's just go a little bit further."

I said, "I can't continue on this road."

But she replied, "You have to. Don't give up. I came to help you."

The road became worse—muddier and muddier. It was covered with stones mixed with mud. I said, "Mother, let's face it, we can't walk on this road anymore."

My mother said, "Oh no, we are not going to give up. We are going to go back and take the car."

"But, Mother, you have never driven a car in your life. How are you going to drive a car?"

"Leave it up to me. I can solve it."

My mother disappeared with my knapsack and purses. I called after her, "Where are you? Don't go, Mother! You're going to perish. Even I cannot go."

Then, I could see my mother coming, driving a car. I couldn't believe my eyes. She opened the car door and said, "Hop in. I already placed your stuff inside. It's going to be a lot easier to go with the car."

I said, "Mother, you've never driven in your whole life!"

"Leave it up to me. I can handle it. You know I handled many things in my life. Didn't I handle the loss of your father by getting a job in order to survive? Before the war when your father was alive, I didn't have to work. I was a housewife. I only had to take care of my family—you and your father."

So, somehow, I had confidence in my mother. I thought, *My mother is a strong-willed person and she manages to come out of the most difficult situations. Maybe she has a point.* So I got into the car and my mother stepped on the gas pedal and drove off. I couldn't believe it—she started driving faster and faster. I cried, "Mother, slow down or we are going to have an accident!"

I could see a car parked at a small distance from us. I said, "Slow down, Mother, or you are going to bump into that car!"

She slowed down, but unfortunately we bumped into the car. We didn't hit the car too hard, but, nevertheless, we did bump the car and there were people in it. "You see, Mother, you should not have driven. What are we going to do now? You don't have a license. We have to call the police."

She said, "Leave it up to me. I can handle it."

I wondered how my mother was going to handle the situation this time. Then I saw some people coming out of the car who looked Italian: a man, his wife, and two children. The man approached, angry and upset. He asked, "How old is this woman?"

I answered, "My mother is ninety-three."

He asked, "Does she have a license?"

I said, "No."

"You let your ninety-three-year-old mother drive without a license? Couldn't you drive yourself? Aren't you ashamed?" He wanted to call the police. I didn't know if there even was a police station nearby.

Then my mother said to me, "Let me handle this."

I said, "Mother, I don't know how you're going to handle this because now we are going to get in deep trouble. My license can be revoked because I let you drive without a license. We're going to end up at the police station."

She got out and approached the Italian man. To my surprise, the man said, "Ah, you are Mrs. Mozes! (My maiden name was Mozes.) We knew your family."

I wondered, *How could they know my family? We were living in Romania, in Transylvania, at that time. How could they know my parents?* Nevertheless, the man said, "We knew your husband. He was such a kind man."

My mother said, "How nice to see you," and they started conversing. My mother introduced me. She said, "This is my daughter."

"Ah," they said, "this is your daughter?"

"Yes, I was trying to help her. Maybe I should have slowed down sooner so I wouldn't hit you. I'm really sorry about this."

"Don't feel sorry. We are so happy to see you. Maybe it was meant to happen. If you hadn't bumped into us, we would have never had the opportunity to meet and to talk to you like this."

They started talking again like old friends. Anyway, nothing much happened and then they said goodbye. The man stepped into his car and drove away with his family. Then my mother said to me, "You see, I could handle the situation. You've also handled many situations in your life. Why do you have such difficulty in continuing to walk on this road?"

"Mother, I am tired. Somehow I have no motivation, no desire to go on."

But she insisted, "You have to do it."

She then got out of the car and took my two purses and knapsack. "Look ahead," she said, "don't you see the road has changed? We traveled together on the hardest part of it."

Indeed, there was a beautiful paved road in front of me. I couldn't understand how this road, that was muddy and filled with stones and so difficult to pass, had suddenly become smooth. "I can't understand, Mother. How did this happen?"

My mother answered, "Can I tell you a little secret?"

"Yes, Mother."

"This road wasn't as bad as you thought."

"I've only seen mud and stones."

"Yes, but I have seen something else. This road is a path to the place you really wanted to go. This was just a hard passage in your life. I knew it was hard for you and that's why I came to help. But from now on you can handle it on your own."

"Mother, my load is so heavy and I don't know what I put in these purses. I feel so tired."

She said, "Your load isn't so heavy anymore. Just try it."

She was right and I exclaimed, "How come it seems so much lighter now? Why did it seem so heavy before?"

"Because you needed a little help to lighten your load and I came to your assistance."

"Mother, would you like to stay with me? I want you to stay with me. You've been away for so long, I missed you."

"I might have been away from you for a long time, but you didn't realize that my spirit was always beside you. I knew exactly, at all times, what you were doing. How else would I know you needed my help?"

I felt that, indeed, my mother had a point. Then suddenly it struck me: *My mother died! This is her spirit, and her spirit is always watching over me.*

She looked at me and smiled, "You are right, I know what you are thinking. It is very true. Goodbye, my child."

She disappeared. I woke up in my bedroom, and my eyes filled up with tears. The picture of my mother, as always, was on my dresser. I picked up her picture, looked at her, gave her a kiss, and said, "Mother, I know that the spirit never dies. You always told me that, but now I truly believe it."

That was one of my dreams about my mother, but then a year later I had another dream about her. Her spirit came to me again. In my first dream she probably wanted to remind me that no matter how many difficulties we encounter in life, we still have to go on and have the hope that we can overcome our obstacles and difficulties. But in my second dream, my mother had another message for me—one that I will keep in mind for the rest of my life.

I dreamed that I was in a big space outdoors, and there was some celebration going on. Somebody came to me and said, "Do you see all these people gathered here?"

I asked, "What kind of celebration is this?"

He said, "Oh, this is not a celebration. These people are coming to hear you speak."

"To hear me speak? What about?"

"You are a public speaker, you are a poet. They heard about you and they want to listen to your poetry recital. They also want to hear your thoughts on life."

I saw the people gathered and I was just about to start my presentation, when everyone looked at me. I began: "Life and death are the two inseparable components of man's destiny. Each day somewhere the birth of a new life is celebrated, and each day somewhere the mourners close the eyes of those who depart from this world forever." I began to recite my poem "Prologue."

Prologue

Life is but a brief encounter
With the joys of earthly fun—
On the wheel of fate
Our destiny is spun—
Delicate strands of ecstasy
Mixed with coarse fibers of doom and agony
Are woven on the loom of existence
By the invisible hands of Almighty God—
The finished cloth,
Stamped with our blood,
Never becomes our property—
We are allowed only
To take a short glimpse
Of its beauty,
Before death takes it away
At the end of our last day—

After my recital I started talking about life and death. "Life is the greatest miracle created by God, and the most precious gift entrusted to humanity to be cherished and respected. What is death? Death is the ultimate fate of man." As I was finishing the phrase, I could see my mother coming. At that moment I was so shocked I couldn't utter a word. I knew my mother had come to listen to me and to talk to me. In my dream, I realized that it was only her spirit coming to meet me because I was aware that she wasn't alive anymore. I could see that she had some difficulty finding me because of the crowd.

She was dressed in her favorite beige-colored spring coat. She lived in Israel for many years and it was purchased there. Many times I wanted to get her a new spring coat, but she wanted only that one, partly because it was from Israel. She got that coat when she was much younger. In my dream Mother appeared so much younger than at the time of her death. She had hardly any gray hair. She looked to be about forty-four, the age she was when I found her upon my return from the German concentration camps. She was a very beautiful woman, possessing a striking combination of a light complexion and wavy black hair.

I desperately wanted to talk to her, so when she spotted me, I ran towards her. The crowd was surprised that I interrupted my recital but I didn't care. I was trying to get to my mother and meet her. It wasn't an easy situation because there were so many people that it seemed an impossibility to get through the big assembly. But in my dream, it felt like I was floating towards her. The crowd was making space for me to get to her, and my mother was approaching from the opposite direction.

All the way I thought, *What will I say to my mother when I meet her? I hope I will have enough time to tell her all my thoughts, how much I miss her and how much I love her.* Finally, at one point we reached each other and embraced. I held onto her like a fruit to a tree but to my great surprise, I couldn't say a single word! I found no words for the love and happiness I felt in seeing her. My mother couldn't say a single word either. We just held each other. But there was a spiritual communication between us. I understood that we were both saying, "I love you, I love you, I love you." But there was a message beyond that. Although my mother did not speak, I could feel what she wanted to say, "Preserve the love in your heart. I will always love you, my spirit is always with you."

I wanted to say, "Mother, I miss you, I love you." And she also understood my thoughts. Finally, I realized that the crowd was looking at me and probably thinking I was insane. There I stood, holding and hugging somebody whom they didn't see. Then I asked my mother, "Can anyone see you?"

She answered, "No, no, my child, nobody can see me except you, because this is my spirit that is with you."

I thought, *Oh dear, what impression do I make here as a speaker? Everyone is looking at me like I am crazy*. On the other hand, I felt, *I don't care. If anyone thinks I am insane, if anyone goes away and they don't come back anymore to listen to me, I don't care because I am holding my mother—she is here with me. This is more important.*

At that point I woke up, and even in my waking state I could feel that my mother was still with me. I knew that her spirit was always with me. Ever since, I have felt that her spirit follows me and watches over me.

I've also had other dreams about my mother. Once I dreamed she was very ill and she was lying in bed with her eyes closed. She wasn't conscious, and looked just as I had seen her on her deathbed. I was holding her hand. In my dream, I did not remember that she had died. But I was aware of the terrible feeling that she was dying. As my husband is a physician, I went to him and said, "Come and help my mother; she seems to be unconscious. I want to talk to her and perhaps you can help her by giving her some medication."

My husband came in, looked at her, and said, "There is no medication for that. Your mother is dying. She is unconscious. She can't talk to you anymore no matter how much you desire it. You have to accept that there is a time when everyone has to go from this earth."

But I could not accept that. I was sitting by her bed, and I said, "Mother, I want to talk to you. Please don't die, I want to have you around. You have been my single parent through all these years. Please talk to me, I know you are not dead yet."

There was a silence, but then my mother opened her eyes and looked at me. She said, "It's true, I'm not dead yet, but I am dying."

"Oh, Mother, please don't die. Please live a little longer, I love you so! I don't want to lose you."

"My child, don't cry, someday we all must go."

"No, Mother, no, I want you to stay longer."

"Look, I am sick, I am bedridden. I am not like I used to be. If you truly love me, you have to let me go. Life has no meaning for me anymore."

"Mother, I want you to live for me."

"I will always be with you, even if I die."

'Mother, how can you be with me after you die? You are going to be buried in the ground and I will never see you. Then I won't be able to touch you, to embrace you."

"My body may lie deep in the ground, but my spirit will always follow you around."

Then my mother closed her eyes.

I said, "Mother, Mother, wake up!" But there was no answer. Then I heard a voice in the room. It was hers.

"I am at peace now. Accept the things you cannot change. My spirit will always be with you. From now on we are going to communicate only on a spiritual level. Goodbye, my child, be at peace with yourself. If you truly love me, you will let me go. You don't want me to suffer any longer."

I realized that my mother was right—I didn't want her to suffer any longer. It would be very wrong for me to demand that. I embraced my mother on her deathbed. She fell into a deep coma and didn't talk to me anymore, but I hugged and kissed her while tears ran down my cheeks. I felt such a great emotional pain—a terrible feeling of loss within my soul that words cannot describe. At that point I woke up and the tears were still running down my cheeks. I thought, *My mother is dead, but in my dream her message to me was again the same as in all my dreams: "The spirit never dies."*

So I know that her spirit will always be with me. I lost her physical body, but not her spirit. We are the children of God; we carry within us the spark of eternity.

The physical body of my father was also lost, just like my mother's. But his spirit will live with me forever, too. After all, I am a part of him. He died many years ago in the German concentration camps. He was a victim of the Holocaust, just like I almost was, and just like many of my other family members. Some six-million Jewish people were also the victims of the Holocaust.

How can I ever forget my father? He was a gentle man, who believed in the power of words and not in the power of blows. He taught me to have love for mankind, to have compassion in my heart, to respect my parents and my grandparents. He also encouraged me to have a goal, to be a professional person, to further my education. He was the one who instilled in me the desire to go to medical school. Circumstances didn't allow me to finish medical school; things change in life, and many times we change with the circumstances. War creates a lot of havoc in every person's life. War creates destruction. I hope there will be a time when there will be peace on earth, although I doubt it, because greed and thirst for power are built into humans, it seems.

But my father was a peace-loving man and he had a great love for his family. He never had to tell me in words what love is because he demonstrated it in each of his actions. He was a hardworking man and had a heart of gold. He demonstrated so much thoughtfulness and affection towards my mother and me—I was an only child, he loved us dearly. I remember what he said to me when we were separated in Auschwitz-Birkenau, "Follow the path of love, forgiveness, and tolerance." I promised him that I would always fulfill his wish. I know that his spirit is with me, just like my mother's spirit. Many times, in my dreams, I don't even remember that he's dead.

Several years ago, I had a dream about him. In many of my dreams about him, he leaves a message behind, which I always hold in my heart. It stays with me for the rest of my life. I think of him very often.

In that particular dream, I was in a big ballroom filled with people. I wondered why they were dressed so informally for this occasion. Generally women wear dresses and men wear suits. And although there were so many people present, there wasn't even a dance floor where people could dance. The whole ballroom was packed with people. I asked myself, *Who are these people? I don't know anyone. Why did I come here?* I didn't even know if I had an invitation, or why I was in that place at all.

Then as I looked around, trying to find some familiar faces, I could see my father walking in. He was at the far end of this huge, crowded room. I was so happy to see him—he looked so young, just as he was before he was taken to the German concentration camps. He was forty-seven years old at that time, and he always looked younger than his age. When I was a teenager and I was walking with my father, people thought he was a suitor because he looked so young. He was a competitive fencer, also trained by my Uncle Eugene, who was a fencing champion of Romania. Uncle Eugene inspired my father to participate in competitions. Because of his training, my father was always in excellent shape. He was a slender and handsome man. I wondered why he was wearing his favorite winter coat, considering that the ballroom had a warm temperature. He loved that winter coat. It had a little mini-fur on the collar.

I grew up in the northern part of Transylvania, which is part of Romania at the present time. At the time of our deportation, it was part of Hungary. Our city, Cluj, was the capital of Transylvania, and was surrounded by the Carpathian Mountains and the Transylvania Alps. Because of that we had quite a cold climate. We had very harsh winters, and short summers. The snow didn't melt from November until the end of March. We had beautiful lakes on which I ice skated.

My father was always cold in winter; he suffered from the cold. He had this nice, wool winter coat with a fur collar. At that time there were not many cars so he walked to his office. During the winter he would usually come into the house snow-covered, his fur collar pulled up to his face and a fur cap on his head.

When he came home from work, he was always carrying something for me, usually some chocolates or candy. When I was a very young child, sometimes it seemed to me that he hadn't brought me anything. But then he would tell me to check his pockets, and I would always find some small presents there. He taught me what love is. I remember the greatest lesson in love he gave me when I was just three years old. It was my mother's birthday; I went to my father and said, "Daddy, I need money."

"What do you need money for?"

"Because it is Mother's birthday and I want to get her a present."

"You don't need money for the nicest and most precious present you can get."

"What present can you get without money?"

He smiled, "You can give your mom a present that no money can buy."

I asked, "What can you buy without money?"

He answered, "The Gift of Love. Go to your mom, embrace her, and give her a big kiss. Tell her, 'Mom, I love you.'"

I did that. I went to my mom, I hugged her and I said, "Mom, I love you, I love you," and I gave her a kiss. I thought, *I gave the greatest, most precious present on earth to my mom and I didn't need any money for it; I gave her the Gift of Love.* Indeed, love cannot be bought with money. That was my first big lesson in love coming from my father.

So … in my dream I saw my father come in with his winter coat on, the fur collar was pulled up to his face and he had a fur cap on his head. He was searching for me. When I spotted him, I prayed to God he should look at me. I asked myself, *How is he going to find me among all these people?* I decided to put my attention on him by constantly looking at him. After awhile, he looked my way and our eyes met. We tried to reach each other, but the room was filled with people. Only in a dream can you push all the obstacles aside and run to each other. The people were making way for us. They moved aside. Suddenly, I wasn't aware of anyone else. I could see only my father coming towards me, and I was rushing towards him.

All the way, just like in the dreams about my mother, I was thinking, *What will I say to my father when I meet him?* I wanted to tell him so many things. I hadn't seen him for so long, there were so many things happening in my life. Finally, we reached each other and embraced. I felt that my father was so cold, but then, it hit me that my father had come from a cold place … my father was dead … but, he looked so alive!

As we embraced, I could feel him grow warmer. I wanted to warm him up and make him feel comfortable. We hugged for a long time. I felt such a tremendous love emanating from him. The same great love was radiating from me, and I felt intense joy in seeing him. Just like in the dream about my mother, we couldn't say a word to each other. Again, we were communicating on a spiritual level, where you have no words, but your feelings are conveyed. I felt a message coming from him, "I love you, I love you," but also another message came along with it, "Don't ever let love desert your heart. Always have love in your heart, not only for your family but for every creature in the world. Have respect for life."

Tears ran down my cheeks, and I could see the tears running down from his eyes also. Then, I woke up. I opened my eyes, and the dream was gone, but the feeling was still there. The words which were not spoken were etched into my soul. Then, I thought, *If I had been able to talk to my father in my dream, what would I have said to him? And further, if we had been able to talk, what would he have said to me?*

I got up and put on my morning robe. I went to my desk, picked up my pen and paper, and I wrote down this dialogue containing the thoughts and feelings which were unspoken in my dream, the words which manifested themselves in the waking state. This is what I would have told my father had I been able to speak to him in my dream. Here are the words he would have said to me while we hugged. Everything is conveyed here in my poem.

In Your Memory

Many years ago
A wise man told me:
"Wherever you go, my thoughts will follow—
When pain will grab your soul,
Or sorrow squeeze your heart,
Think of me and you will never fall apart …
My love for you will never die!

I may be soaring above in the blue kingdom of the sky,
My body may be sealed beneath the earth,
But remember,
I shared and witnessed your birth—
I will never desert you!
I will watch over you when you are awake or asleep,
I will listen to your voice,
I will weep when you suffer,
And laugh when you rejoice."

O, wise man, I know you speak the truth—
I left the border of youth,
Standing on the stage of maturity,
Wearing the gray signs
And the dry lines of age.
I understand now
All the teachings
You bestowed upon me
Through the years—
Since you left me
My eyes shed countless drops of tears.
My dear father,
How can I thank you
For all the years of love,
Wisdom, guidance and care?
How can I ever bear
Your absence?
I always feel your presence—
For me you never died.
I see you in my dreams

Floating in life's streams—
You are here with me,
We never are apart.
Death could never tear you out of my heart—
Wherever your mortal body rests
May be death's domain,
But your spirit will always remain
Buried within me.

My dear father,
Wherever you may be—
Under the cold rocks
Or behind a shining star,
I am with you
Wherever you are!
My thoughts will hold forever your image,
And in my eternal pilgrimage,
My quest to reach your soul
Will be my highest goal.

Many times I also dreamed about my uncle, who had a great love for me. As I mentioned before, he didn't have any children. I was his little girl and I can thank him that I returned from the German concentration camps alive, because he taught me to be strong. Many times he said, "It's good to have spiritual strength, but you need the physical strength along with it." He was so right. I am glad I was a competitive fencer, that I started fencing when I was five-years old, and that I worked up great endurance so I could survive the German concentration camps. I learned the value of spirituality and of physical fitness. I consider myself fortunate to have had two such wonderful men in my family, my father and my uncle, who gave me such a great heritage and great values in life. They pointed out to me the supreme value of love and instilled compassion and tolerance in my heart. But they also taught me the importance and the benefits of physical fitness.

Several years ago I had a strange dream about my uncle. I know that his spirit is also with me.

In my dream I was at Miami beach, and I was deliberating why I had gone there. I was by myself and I wondered where my husband and my family were, because I remembered that we had gone there together. But on that day I found myself alone on Miami beach, and I looked at the sidewalk next to the seashore. It was a walkway made out of wood, and it had a fence around it, too. I had been to Miami beach before, but I had never seen this kind of setting.

Then, on the wooden platform, I could see my uncle coming towards me. He was a handsome man, very athletically built. In my dream, he was still the well-built Olympic athlete. Strangely, though, he was covered with mud. My uncle was normally a very neat man; he took pride in his appearance. He always wanted to give a good example of being strong, well-built physically. He was a neat, intelligent man, very ambitious and courageous.

When I saw him, it seemed to me that his spirit was somewhat broken. He moved slowly. He usually walked vigorously at a fast pace. Now, here he was covered with mud. I pondered, *What happened to my uncle? Where has he been?* I never had seen him looking like this. He came along the walkway, stopped, and faced me. I was so happy to see him. Again, as in so many of my dreams, I did not realize he was dead. I wondered where he came from, and why he had so much dirt on him.

He looked at me, and I said, "I'm so glad to see you! I haven't seen you for years. You never came to see me."

He stopped and said, "I did come to see you. I was looking for you."

"How did you know that I was here?"

"I know more than you think. I'm always with you." Then, as he was standing on that platform, the fence disappeared, and he walked up to me.

"Uncle, I am so happy to see you." I embraced him even though he was covered with mud. Little did I care. I said, "Tell me, where were you through all these years? How did you get into this mess?"

"Do you want to find out? Then come with me."

So we walked together. Suddenly Miami beach completely disappeared and we walked on a barren surface for awhile. Then, I could see from afar a single, beautiful, huge tree. I followed my uncle and we came to a place where the only appealing thing was that tree. Everything looked so barren, so desolate. It was a muddy road. As we went on that muddy road, we came to a place where there were rectangular holes in the ground that looked like beds of mud.

My uncle said to me, "That's where I live."

"How could you live in such a place? Why did you choose to live here?"

"I had no choice. Do you want to see where my place is? See that big tree? That's the only attractive thing around me. I was fortunate to have my place by the trunk of the tree."

"Uncle, it's terrible, I want to take you away from here. Don't live here. It's like a mudhole."

"You can call it a mudhole, but this is where I have to live forever."

"Why? You can come with me."

"Don't you understand that I cannot come with you? This is where I sleep. This is where I rest, and I have rested here for a long time."

"What is it like to live in a place like this?"

"Do you really love me?"

"You know, I always loved you! I will love you even if you live in this mudhole. I don't care. I want to understand you. Why do you live here? What does it feel like to live here in this big isolated place? It looks so sad, dead, and desolate."

"It does. You want to know what it is really like? Do you love me enough to want to really understand what it feels like to live here?

"Yes."

"Then you have to do something for me. See this mudhole next to me? You have to lie down and feel what it is like to lie in this mud. I will lie next to you, and you can tell me what you feel."

Surely I was reluctant to do that, but I loved my uncle dearly and I would do anything for him. So I lay down there. Naturally I was covered with mud, and it was cold, uncomfortable, and messy.

"What does it feel like?"

"Uncle, if you really love me you have to get away from here."

"You still don't know what it feels like and what I have to put up with here."

"With what?"

"Do you love me? Do you want to find out?"

"Yes."

"Then you have to stay here until nightfall."

Again, I was very reluctant to do that, but I wanted to find out what happened at nightfall. *What does my uncle want to relate to me? What is it?* I lay next to my uncle, and we talked.

"Do you still like to fence? I was so proud of you. Remember when you won that little gold medal, and you were fencing with boys? When you were twelve years old and your breasts were growing, you said, 'Uncle, I cannot fence anymore, it hurts.' Do you recall when I got you that extra padding for your chest? I also taught you to fence with the foil because the saber was too harsh for you."

"I do remember."

"I was proud of you, so proud of you."

We talked more and I told him all that had happened to me through the years, including my experiences in the German concentration camps.

"I'm so glad that you survived, because do you realize I didn't, and your father didn't?"

In that moment I realized that my uncle was dead, and this was his grave. I experienced the coldness of the grave, the ultimate fate of man, and I was terrified. I shivered from the cold.

"Don't be afraid, I want to give you a message. I want you to learn something about death."

Then, when nightfall came, I could see the sinister-looking swordsmen coming out of the darkness, wearing the masks of death. I wondered if they were the representatives of death. They were coming towards me. I had no defense against them.

"Uncle, am I going to die? Am I going to join you? Is this death coming to take my life?"

"Don't be afraid."

In that moment my uncle stepped out of the grave, and suddenly there was no mud on him anymore, but he held the saber in his hand. He was dressed in his fencing uniform, the fencing shield on his head, since he was fencing champion of Romania. I watched him challenge the shadows of death; he fenced with the dark specters of oblivion.

"Uncle, you can't win! There are too many!"

"Don't be afraid, don't be afraid. I am going to be the winner. I challenged death before; I fight with death every single night. This is my life here."

Then my uncle started fencing with all the shadows of death and defeating them. Every single one fell on the ground. He was still dressed in his fencing uniform like I had seen him in the competitions. He won so many competitions; he had so many medals and all kinds of trophies.

"Uncle, I admire you even in death. I always admired you, but I never thought that you could challenge death. You are the greatest fencer on Earth."

He stood before me, "Get up."

He started cleaning me, and all the mud and dirt disappeared.

"Uncle, now I understand that you are destined to stay here and continue fencing with the most fearsome and powerful opponents. In the domain of death, each day you face the toughest competitors. Your greatest challenge is death itself."

"Now you see why I stay here. This is the only thing I like here, to fence with the specters of death. I don't know if I will always be victorious, but constantly I will fight with them and I will try my best to be the winning champion of the dead. Your place isn't here, but I wanted you to understand me. I know that you have mourned for me throughout many years. I want you to leave and know that I am not totally unhappy. But there is something I want to tell you before I leave. Remember, don't be afraid wherever you are, and wherever you are going to be. You should know that the spirit of your uncle is always with you, to protect you, to fight for you and to guide you, even beyond the grave. Now, let's go back together."

He took my hand, and we walked hand-in-hand. I looked up at him.

"Uncle, I love you, I love you! I knew through all these years that your spirit was always with me."

"I love you, too. My spirit will always follow you. I may be deep in the ground, but my spirit will always be around you."

Then he disappeared. I stood alone on the beach for a long time, by the front of the wooden platform. After the fence disappeared, the whole platform gradually vanished. Then, I woke up and I felt such a terrible sadness, such an indescribable feeling of loss. It felt like a part of me was gone.

I thought of my dear uncle. The pictures of my uncle, of my father, and of my mother are hanging on the bedroom wall facing my bed. There is also a picture of me with my mother and my father when I was five-years old. I hung these pictures in such a way that when I go to bed, I can look at them. They're enlarged photos so I can see clearly the faces of my loved ones.

As I woke up, my eyes fell on the pictures and I knew that their spirits were there in my room. And I knew they were going to stay with me. Their spirits are alive in my soul, their spiritual resting place, and they will be with me as long as there is life within me.

You never overcome the loss of your loved ones. You mourn them forever. But it is a comforting feeling that they are with you. You can feel them although you cannot see them. There is a sensation, a feeling that they are there and they read your thoughts, and they sometimes manifest themselves in your dreams. Those magical dreams are the only place where you can see them and communicate with them, an experience which is always precious to me.

Message from Heaven

An angel sent from Heaven
Appeared at my side.
Her white wings were spread out wide,
Her body was wrapped in a golden veil.
She looked so delicate but strong, not frail.
Her friendly face reflected
So much charm, kindness and grace.
By looking at this saintly apparition
Coming from out of space,
A calm feeling descended upon me.
She brought to my heart
The bright rays of the sun.
Suddenly all my anxieties and fears were gone.

Then gradually she stepped forward,
Stopping in front of me,
Holding in her hand
A square-shaped tablet
Carved out of precious stone.
She looked at me silently.
I felt shivers going through
My every bone.
She addressed me kindly,
Her voice was pleasant and clear.
It was like soft music
Coming to my ear.

I was sent here
To bring you a message
From above.
I am the angel
Of Faith, Hope and Love.
Read the text
Engraved on this sacred tablet
And let your mind be absorbed
In the content featured
On that ethereal board.

I looked at the sacred object
Placed in front of my eyes,
Sent to me from Heaven's Paradise.
The following inscription
Was carved with utter perfection
In fancy, bold letters
By Divine Invisible Fingers:

Mortal, upon you I call.
If attaining happiness is your goal,
Then don't be an enemy
But, be a friend of your soul.

Let the clock of time
Strike for you the happy hours.
Compare your life not to grime,
But to beautiful, blooming flowers.

Have faith and trust in your Creator,
Your Guide and Protector.
Place yourself into His hands.
He will take good care of you
And all your wishes will come true.

Be a genuine believer
And God will deliver
All the help you need,
With utmost speed.
The assistance will also come
From the angels above.
If you practice the art of forgiveness,
Faith, hope and love,
You will then find peace,
And all your worries,
Doubts and fears will cease.
So don't whine and brood,
But change your somber mood.
Start your day with a smile,
Not with a tear,
With courage and no fear.

Remember that your maiden name is Mozes.
You carry a sacred Biblical title
From the Old Testament,
Associated with liberation and sacrament.

Therefore, stop your tears and lament,
Be happy and content.
You survived the fires of the Holocaust.
My blessings upon you I cast.
You passed many of the hard tests
I subjected you to,
And you will also pass through
The present one, too.
Be patient and strong
And remember your tight bond
With your Creator,
Who listens to your prayer,
Who is always at your side
To be your Counselor and Guide.
So be in peace.
All your worries and doubts
Will soon cease.

Send to Me a note of reply
To the distant sky
With My saintly messenger,
And control your frustration and anger.

The angel was standing by,
Waiting for my reply.
I ran into my den,
Picked up paper and pen,
And completed my letter,

Conveying in it my most intimate thoughts,
And my unsuccessful dealings
With my disturbing feelings.

O God, my Creator,
Thank You for Your message
From Heaven's Kingdom.
Give me the ability
To apply to my life
All the principles of wisdom.
Save me from emotional weakness
And from physical sickness.
Grant me the ability
To see clearly
The responsibility towards myself.

King of the Universe and Man,
Help me to give
All the love I can
To my family and mankind,
And to leave all my depressing thoughts behind.

Perform on me the miracle
Of spiritual regeneration
And feed my mind
With Divine Inspiration.
Guide me to explore the depth of my soul.
Assist me to find my true mission and goal.
Please grant me the ability
To become the writer and composer

I was meant to be,
And let me disperse the wonders and beauty
Of the Universe
Through my music and verse.

Almighty, help me to maintain my strengths,
Patience and tolerance,
Through the entire length of my existence.
Bestow upon me the attributes
Of resilience and persistence.
O Lord, I worship and glorify Thee,
And I love Thee with all my heart,
My spirit and my body.

The angel picked up my letter,
Opened her broad wings,
And flew high up into the sky
Without even saying goodbye.

I stood in amazement,
Wondering if what I had experienced
Was only a vision, a strange dream,
Or was it reality,
Or maybe just an unexplainable mystery.

About the Author

Magda Herzberger was born and raised in the city of Cluj, Romania. She is a poet, lecturer, composer, and the author of eight previously published books: *The Waltz of the Shadows* (1st and 2nd Editions); *Eyewitness to Holocaust*; *Will You Still Love Me?*; *Songs of Life*; and her most recent works, *Survival*, the compelling autobiography of Magda's early life in Romania and her suffering at the hands of the Nazis; *Devotional Poetry*, dedicated to the readers of *Survival*; *Tales of the Magic Forest*; and *If You Truly Love Me*, dedicated to her husband on their 60th wedding anniversary.

Magda was a marathon runner, skier, and mountain climber. She and her husband, Dr. Eugene Herzberger, a retired neurosurgeon, reside in Fountain Hills, Arizona. They have a daughter Monica, a son Henry, and two grandchildren.

Magda's primary goals are to instill love for poetry in the hearts of people through her work, to keep the memory of the Holocaust alive, and to show the beauty of life through her writings and music. Her philosophy of life: Have faith, hope, and love in your heart—believe in impossible dreams and make them come true—cherish each moment of life—and never take anything for granted.

Groundbreaking Press, publisher of *Dreamworld*, *If You Truly Love Me*, and *Survival*, also publishes the Second Edition of *The Waltz of the Shadows*, *Devotional Poetry*, and her first children's book, *Tales of the Magic Forest.*

Magda may be contacted at:
magdaherzberger@yahoo.com
www.magdaherzberger.com

About the Illustrator

The cover and interior illustrations for *Dreamworld* have been created by Monica A. Wolfson. Monica is Magda Herzberger's daughter. She also created the cover and inside illustrations for Magda's books, *Devotional Poetry*, *Tales of the Magic Forest*, and *If You Truly Love Me.*

Monica has a Masters from Arizona State University in Educational Technology. She is also an accomplished singer, having performed in various venues, and having written and published her own songs and poetry. In addition to all of the above, she is a professional photographer.

Monica is married to Dave Wolfson, a transportation planner and committed storm chaser and photographer. They live in Fountain Hills, Arizona.

Monica can be contacted at:
monica@wolfsonworks.com
www.wolfsonworks.com

www.ingramcontent.com/pod-product-compliance
Lightning Source LLC
LaVergne TN
LVHW091034080826
845145LV00002B/491